CYNTHIA HICKEY

Calm Surface
Misty Hollow, Book 3

Cynthia Hickey

ISBN: 978-1-956654-19-6

To all those who love a page-turning romantic suspense.

Chapter One

Maddy Everton inserted the key into the lock of the house that had once belonged to her sister, Allison. Tears sprang to her eyes. Only a month had passed since Allison's murder, her body discovered in Lake Misty, and the house already smelled of mildew.

"Don't worry, little sister. I'll find out who did this to you." Maddy headed back to her car to unload the suitcases from the trunk.

When she'd received the call from the Misty Hollow police department that her sister's body had been discovered, she'd quit her job in Oak Ridge and taken a teaching job in Misty Hollow. She hadn't thought twice about coming to find out what had happened to Alli.

Who would want to kill such a sweet girl? At twenty-three, her sister had come to this town on a quest for independence. A town where she could forge her own life. The last time Maddy had spoken to her, Alli had been over the moon about her new job at the local library. She'd used her inheritance from their parents to purchase the little two-bedroom house in town that would now be Maddy's home for however long it took.

She heaved the largest suitcase from the trunk and glanced around. On each side of her was a white house with a wraparound porch. Country charm that belied a town that housed evil. Oh, she knew of the troubles Misty Hollow had had in the past. She'd done her research before coming. Sweet and peaceful, seemingly calm, but this hidden little town could be a cauldron of trouble.

A quick glance at her watch alerted her that she'd arrived later than she'd wanted. That was her, Miss Perpetually Late. Meet the teacher night at the school started in four hours, and she still hadn't prepared her classroom. She slid the suitcases just inside the front door, then sped to the local elementary school.

"You must be Madison Everton." A smiling woman a few years older than Maddy pulled a box from Maddy's trunk. I'm Susan Snodgrass. I also teach fifth grade. You'll want to check in with the principal and secretary before heading to your room. Meanwhile, I can ask the maintenance man to unload your car for you."

"Really?" Maddy grinned. "That would be great. I've just arrived in town."

"Wow. You're really pushing it."

"Yep." She rushed into the building, greeted everyone she needed to greet, then got hopelessly lost trying to find her room. "Ah. Room 105." As promised, all her boxes sat in her room. She wouldn't have time to set up the room exactly as she wanted it, but she'd make a good effort.

A man in navy-blue coveralls leaned against her

door frame. His eyes narrowed. "Everton? You related to the girl the police just found in the lake?"

Maddy stiffened. "I'm her sister. You are?"

"Gene Howard. Site specialist. Welcome to Misty Hollow. I hope you find what you're looking for. But I also hope you aren't bringing trouble with you." Before she could thank him for bringing in her boxes, he left.

Despite his greeting, she didn't feel welcomed in the slightest. She quickly slid books into bookcases, slapped up a few encouraging posters, and set out a few personal items on her desk. That's the best she could do. Tomorrow would be more productive as long as meetings didn't fill up all her time.

"Folks are arriving. You ready?" Susan poked her head into the room.

"As ready as I'll ever be." Maddy fought to control her racing heart. She should've arrived in town yesterday, but it had taken longer to find a renter for her apartment in Oak Ridge than she'd thought. She took up position outside her classroom door and pasted on a welcoming smile. As a second-year teacher, she knew the drill.

A handsome man strolled the halls. What made him stand out was the fact he didn't have a student with him. Had the school asked for extra security for that night?

He caught her watching and headed her way. "Hello. You're new."

"Maddy Everton."

A flicker crossed his eyes. "Family to Allison Everton?"

"Her sister." Maddy hitched her chin. "I'm here to find out what happened to her."

His smile faded. "That could be very dangerous, ma'am."

She shrugged, keeping her smile in place as she turned to greet a man and young boy. "Will you be in my class this year? I'm Miss Everton."

The boy nodded.

"Speak up, Danny." The man with him placed a hand on the boy's shoulders. "I'm Ryan Maxwell. This is my nephew, Danny. He lives with me." His gaze flicked to the other man. "Bundt. I didn't know you were working tonight."

"Last minute." Deputy Bundt smirked. "With you off for this event, we're left a bit short-handed."

"Mr. Maxwell, perhaps you and Danny would like to see the room?" she intervened. The tension between the two men could be cut with a chainsaw.

They stepped into her room. Maddy motioned to the seat Danny would be occupying. She'd placed a new notebook and pencil at each desk.

Mr. Maxwell asked the same question everyone else seemed to ask. "You related to Allison Everton?"

Maddy exhaled heavily. "Yes, sir. I'm her sister." Her gaze clashed with his dark one. "I'm here to find out who killed her."

~

Was the woman insane? He started to say something to that effect but stopped as Danny glanced their way.

When Danny browsed through the books on the shelf, Ryan lowered his voice. "Your sister was murdered, Miss Everton. Let the police handle finding out what happened."

"We know what happened." She crossed her arms.

4

"Someone murdered her after keeping her hidden for a few days, then dumped her in the lake like fish guts."

A harsh but effective analogy. "If you get in the way of the sheriff's department, you will be arrested." He gave her a firm nod, then called for Danny to follow him.

"I think my new teacher will be nice," his nephew said. "She's pretty. Don't you think so?"

Blond ponytail that hung to her waist and flashing hazel eyes? Yes, she was very pretty. She also looked very much like her deceased sister. "I'm sure you'll like it in Misty Hollow."

"Won't you?" Danny glanced up at him. "It's smaller than Langley. You won't get shot at as much. I like the mountain and the lake. It's nice here."

Ryan ruffled the boy's hair. "Good point." Hopefully, the reason Ryan accepted the position with the Misty Hollow sheriff's office would prove wrong. But with the death of pretty, blond Allison and the circumstances surrounding her death, he didn't think so.

They ran into Deputy Bundt again when Danny wanted to see the multi-purpose room. The lawman was speaking with a man in blue coveralls. Another man leaned against a far wall, his sharp gaze on everyone that came into the large room.

Where was that man's kid? Ryan narrowed his eyes, everyone a suspect. Against another wall, someone had set up a long table with cookies and lemonade. Danny made a beeline for the snacks and struck up a conversation with a boy around his age.

The man lounging against the wall looked interested when Miss Everton entered, but the boy Danny spoke to called him, diverting his attention.

Ryan shook off his suspicions. The new teacher was beautiful. Every man in the place glanced her way. That didn't mean one of them was a killer.

Except his belief the killer lived in Misty Hollow had brought Ryan here. He'd bide his time and pray he was wrong.

Miss Everton marched toward Bundt. From her posture, he guessed she was asking questions about the investigation into her sister's death.

"I'll be right over here, Danny. You can see me."

His nephew rolled his eyes. "I'm not a baby."

"No, you're not. Sorry for treating you like one." Ryan joined Bundt and the teacher in time to hear him say he couldn't divulge that information.

"Miss Everton." Ryan squared his shoulders. "I understand your drive to find answers, but you should know that the authorities can't give you much information."

Her lovely eyes darted from one lawman to the other. "I feel as if I'm being ganged up on."

He frowned. "How so?"

"Deputy Bundt and I were having a conversation, then you come over and start issuing orders."

"He *is* the captain," Bundt said with a smirk. "I'm the grunt, along with Deputy Miller."

Ryan knew why the other man disliked him so much. He'd heard how Bundt had been handling the duties of captain before Ryan arrived on the scene. Now, he answered to Ryan, and they'd be spending time together solving the murder of a young woman well-liked by most in Misty Hollow.

"Are you staying in your sister's house, Miss Everton?" He glanced at the teacher.

"Yes. Please call me Maddy. Everyone does. Only the students will call me Miss Everton." She tilted her head. "There's no reason for me to stay anywhere else when my sister's place is vacant." A shadow crossed her features. "There might be something there to help me find out who killed her. Isn't it usually someone who knew the victim?"

"Not necessarily." Especially if Ryan's suspicion was right. Serial killers didn't usually know their victims.

"I'll let you two argue. Have a nice evening, Miss...Maddy." Bundt strode from the room.

"Is he the school resource officer?" Maddy asked. "Otherwise, why would law enforcement be here tonight?"

"Nothing better to do."

She arched a brow. "Things seemed quite hot this time last year."

"You've done your homework."

"Of course. Then, before that, the sheriff and his present wife had their own adventure. Misty Hollow isn't the charming small town people think it is."

"All towns have their share of trouble." *This* woman was going to be trouble. He had no doubt.

~

His hands itched to grab the pretty new teacher. But, he'd have to bide his time. He already had a woman to love and three days to convince her to love him back. He'd taken her from the grocery store two hours ago, then came here.

Not to show up on Meet the Teacher Night would look suspicious. Everyone in town came. The start of a new school year was a party to most of them, even those without children in the school. The people of Misty Hollow grabbed at any chance to break the monotony of routine. From his shady spot in the parking lot, he waited and watched until the blond teacher headed for her car. He'd follow her home, watch her go inside, then head to where his new woman waited for him.

Chapter Two

By the weekend, Maddy needed time off. Not that she'd have a lot of it. Not with lesson plans to be made and papers to grade, but she'd take whatever few hours would be left. She had questions that needed answers.

She'd heard that the local diner in a small town could be a hive of gossip, so she took some of her schoolwork with her to Lucy's. The aroma of brewing coffee and pastries made her mouth water when she entered. Conversations stopped and heads turned. Greetings were called out before patrons returned to their breakfast.

Smiling at Danny who sat with his uncle in a booth near the big front window, Maddy headed for the booth in back where she could spread out her papers without disturbing anyone. A cute teenage girl in a ruffled yellow apron approached her table.

"What can I get for you?" She smiled.

"I'm new here. What do you recommend?"

"The pancakes are to die for. So are the strawberry crepes. You the new teacher?"

9

"I am, and I'll have the crepes and coffee. I've come to…settle my sister's estate. Did you know Allison?"

"Sure. Everybody did. She worked at the library, volunteered at the food bank—a real nice girl. Sorry for your loss." The teenager started to turn away.

"Just a second, please." Maddy almost grabbed the hem of the girl's apron. "Did my sister have a boyfriend? Someone she hung out with?"

"No boyfriend that I know of, but she hung out with the other waitress." She jerked her head toward a redhead waiting on Danny and his uncle. "Her name is Jill. Want me to send her over?"

"That would be great. Thank you." Her sister's friend would be bound to know something. She watched as her server said something to Jill, who glanced Maddy's way, then nodded. Wonderful. Ignoring the frown tossed her way by Captain Maxwell, Maddy opened her backpack and pulled out a stack of papers.

The captain would simply have to get used to the fact that Maddy meant what she'd said. She intended to find out who killed her sister.

By the time breakfast came, delivered by Jill, Maddy was knee-deep in fifth-grade multiplication. She set the papers aside to make room for her meal.

"Amber said you wanted to talk to me." Jill slid into the booth opposite her. "I have a fifteen-minute break."

"Thank you. I was told you and Allison were friends."

Sadness clouded her face. "We hit it off right away."

"Any idea who might have wanted her dead?"

"No one. That's why most folks around here think someone passing through killed her."

"Wouldn't a stranger have been noticed?" Misty Hollow couldn't have more than five thousand people.

She shrugged. "Most likely. My father thinks it's someone local. Someone new to town."

"Are there many?"

"Two new deputies, the maintenance man at the school, a new manager at the grocery store." Her brow furrowed and she drummed her fingers on the table. "I guess it would have to be a man in order to keep Allison for a few days before dumping her, so I won't mention the women. There's a new boy in my senior class as well."

Maddy didn't think a teenaged boy capable of kidnapping and holding a woman before killing her. "Here's my phone number." She jotted down her number on a napkin. "Call me if you think of anything else. Please."

Now, she had a list of suspects. She stared at the back of Captain Maxwell's head, doubting he could be the killer. Too hard to hold a woman captive with a young boy in the house.

She straightened, thinking back on all the crime shows she'd watched as she studied the short list in front of her. Was one of them Addy's killer? Since she needed groceries, that would be her next stop.

After a delicious breakfast, she gathered her things and paid the bill. The captain and his nephew had left sometime before without her noticing. Why did Danny not live with his parents? She shook her head as she headed for her car. It was none of her business. If he wanted her to know, he'd tell her. Just because she was nosing around with regard to Addy didn't mean she needed to know everything about everyone in Misty Hollow.

The local grocery store parking lot held more cars than she'd thought. Good. If the store carried most of what the town residents needed, Maddy would have no need to venture away from the town. The more the people here got to know her, the more likely they'd be willing to talk.

The photo of the manager hanging on the wall made locating him easy. He looked to be around thirty-five, ordinary-looking, a forced smile. Could be that he didn't like the attention. She shrugged. Killers rarely looked like one.

All of the men on her list were ten years or more older than Addy. Maddy didn't think her sister would've dated a man that much older than herself. That ruled out a crime of passion. She bit the inside of her cheek, studied the photo for a few seconds more, then grabbed a cart for her shopping. She still wanted to have time to visit the place Addy's body had been located.

An hour later, she clutched a handful of colorful autumn leaves and stared off the pier at the calm surface of the water. Across the way, the colorful trees reflected off the water's surface. Addy's body had floated right there near the piling and was discovered by an elderly man fishing in a small boat.

"Oh, Addy." Sobs choked her. "If only you could tell me who did this to you."

~

Ryan glanced over from where he cast a fishing

line into the lake in time to see Maddy toss a handful of leaves into the lake before kneeling on the pier. The waning sun's rays highlighted her long ponytail. The sorrow depicted in the slump of her shoulders and rounded back tugged at his heart. That woman ached to find answers. The very same answers he sought for himself. His cousin, Rachel, hadn't deserved to die any more than Allison had.

The difference between them was the fact he was law enforcement. Her nosing around would only get her into trouble. Especially since she fit the unsub's preferred victimology.

"What is Miss Everton doing?" Danny reeled his line in.

"Talking to her sister." Something tugged on his line. "Got one!" He jerked to set the hook, then reeled in a nice bass. "Better get busy, or I'm going to win this."

Danny scowled and cast his line back out. "How can she talk to a dead person? I don't talk to my parents."

"Maybe you should." His nephew harbored a lot of anger over the incident that claimed the lives of his mother and father. "Might make you feel better."

"Nothing will. A monster took them away."

Time would help ease the pain, but the boy wouldn't understand.

Maddy pushed to her feet and turned away from the water. She froze when she caught sight of them. After a moment's hesitation, she headed their way.

"Uncle Ryan caught a big one," Danny said. "We're having a contest to see who catches the biggest fish. Want to try?"

"I haven't fished in years." Red circled her eyes.

"We've another pole if you want to give it a go." Ryan motioned to a pole next to his tackle box. "Loser has to buy ice cream."

"Then I'd better make sure I don't lose." She smiled, chose a lure, and set up her pole. Her beautiful cast proved that even if it had been a while, the woman was familiar with a fishing pole.

"Uncle Ryan said you were talking to your sister." Danny cocked his head. "How do you do that?"

"By thinking of her and saying what I want to say." She audibly cleared her throat.

"Dead people don't talk." He set his mouth in a grim line.

"No, but they're great listeners. Oh." Her eyes widened as her pole dipped. "I've got one." She reeled in a fish a bit bigger than Ryan's.

"Better hurry, Danny, or your allowance will be buying our ice cream." Ryan grinned.

"No way." He reeled and cast again. After several tries, he changed to a lure similar to the one Maddy used. A few minutes later, he reeled in a fish bigger than Ryan's.

"Looks like I'm buying." He reeled in his pole and closed the tackle box. "Will you join us, Maddy?"

"It's suppertime." She frowned.

"We do this every month on the fifteenth, rain or shine, no matter what is going on." He ignored her disapproving look.

"Why?"

"Because the fifteenth is when my mom and dad died." Danny marched to the car.

"I'm sorry." Her eyes widened.

"It's the best thing I could think of to ease the pain of this day." He lifted the tackle box. "Well, are you going to join us?"

She nodded. "I'll follow you. I could use some ice cream for supper today, too."

At the parlor, all three of them carrying their ice cream, Ryan chose a table in the corner where he had a good view of the door and windows. As usual, he scanned the room, a habit he'd developed after Rachel's death. He counted two women other than Maddy who might interest the unsub. He wanted to warn them. Tell them to color their hair. Leave town. Never leave their house.

Although, Rachel had been taken from her home in the middle of the day, not a single neighbor saw a thing.

"Where did you live before Misty Hollow?" Maddy licked the ice cream off her spoon.

Ryan's stomach did a flip. He tore his gaze away from her mouth. "Langley. When the captain position opened up here, I applied and was hired."

"When did Deputy Bundt move here?"

"He was here when I arrived." He glanced at Danny who was engrossed in a cartoon on Ryan's phone. "Don't ask too many questions, Maddy. It's dangerous."

"Is that a warning or a threat?" Her eyes narrowed.

He exhaled heavily. "Just a warning." He wanted to tell her the real reason he'd moved to Misty Hollow, but the fewer people who knew, the better. Which meant, he kept the reason to himself. Not even the sheriff knew.

"You're keeping a secret." She crossed her arms. "I can see it in your eyes."

"Then you're reading me wrong." His gaze flicked to Danny again who now watched them with curiosity.

"What secret?" His nephew asked.

"Your teacher is mistaken." A twitch developed by Ryan's right eye.

Maddy laughed. "You have to tell, Captain." She stood. "Thank you for the fishing and the ice cream. See you Monday, Danny."

The woman would be a thorn in Ryan's side during the investigation, of that he had no doubt.

~

Through binoculars he'd watched Maddy from the opposite side of the lake as she mourned her sister. He'd been a bit surprised when she joined Maxwell and the boy fishing. Most of the people around Misty Hollow thought the captain unfriendly, surly even.

He didn't care for the man one iota. Didn't matter whether the pretty schoolteacher spent time with the captain. He'd still keep his sights on her if his latest failed him. There were plenty of women to love in Misty Hollow.

A few minutes later, he drove toward Oak Ridge and home. In the house, he stood listening, reassuring himself that the basement soundproofing still kept his secret. He locked the door behind him and headed for the basement stairs.

Then, the beautiful sound of soft sobs greeted his ears when he opened the door to steps that led down to his sanctuary. "Don't cry, sweetheart. I'm coming."

Her sobs turned to whimpers. His blood heated as he increased his pace.

Standing over her, he breathed in her scent, closing his eyes, remembering the original woman who wore the perfume he'd sprinkled over his latest. "Do you love me yet?" He'd taken her yesterday, after the other cursed him. No doubt, her body would be located soon.

"I hate you." She screamed, the sound bouncing back from the soundproofing on the walls.

He sighed. This one, too, would fail.

Chapter Three

Susan huffed in the doorway of Maddy's classroom. "I have Danny Maxwell with me." She stepped back to let the boy enter. "He was throwing food in the cafeteria. When I told him to stop, he started yelling at me. The principal wants you to try and handle him before he gets written up."

Maddy frowned. "Have a seat, Danny. This is my prep time, so you will sit there without making a sound."

He screwed up his face and crossed his arms. Dark circles under his eyes provided a sharp contrast to his pale skin. "I'm sleepy."

"I'm sorry to hear that. This is not naptime."

"How are you going to keep me awake?" He plopped in a chair and squeezed his eyes shut.

Maddy shook her head and returned to the task in front of her. If Danny wanted to be belligerent, she'd call his uncle at the first opportunity. Otherwise, if he really was tired, maybe a short nap would improve his attitude.

Ten minutes later, Danny's whimpering drew her

attention away from her lesson plans. He hunched over, his head on the desk, his little body jerking. "Go away," he mumbled.

"Danny?" Maddy moved to his side and gave him a gentle shake. "Wake up, dear."

"What?" He blinked and glanced around.

"You were dreaming. Go wash your face and come right back here. The others will be returning from recess soon." When he headed for the boy's room, Maddy called Ryan.

"Sleeping? He's in bed every night by eight-thirty."

"Not only that, but he was disrespectful to another teacher at lunch."

Ryan sighed. "He has been acting out the last few days. Do I need to come and get him?"

"Not at the moment. I wanted you to be aware. Oh, and before I woke him, he told someone to go away. In his sleep." She toyed with a pencil on her desk. "Something is bothering him. The death of his parents?"

"Most likely. I'll talk to him, but I really don't know what to do. It's been six months."

"How did they die?"

"They were murdered during a break-in. Danny slept upstairs during the whole thing. He found them the next morning."

Her heart clenched. "Have you considered therapy?"

"I'm looking into it. Thank you. I'll be there to pick him up after school." Click.

Okay, then. Summarily dismissed, Maddy turned her attention to Danny who returned from the

19

bathroom, his shirt wet. "Here." She motioned to a seat next to her desk. "Before the other students return, I want to let you know that you can talk to me about anything."

"Even monsters?" His eyes widened.

"Most definitely about monsters." She would need to find a way to help this child. His uncle tried—she felt that he did—but being a captain might have him stretched too thin when it came to caring for a damaged child. "Are you seeing monsters?"

He gave a slow, deliberate nod. "Outside the house."

"At night?"

"It walks back and forth in front of the trees."

"On two legs or four?" Her mouth dried, her heart seizing.

"Two," he whispered.

The arrival of the rest of the class disrupted any further questions. Maddy sent a quick text to Ryan asking that he stick around at the end of the school day. She had something important to discuss with him. Thinking better of that, she informed him that she would bring Danny home to discuss something important. If her fear was correct, Ryan would want to investigate the "monster." The only monster Maddy believed in was human.

She kept a close eye on Danny the rest of the day. He seemed more subdued than he'd been during her prep time. Every few minutes, he glanced toward the window. Situated too high in the wall for the students to be distracted by what went on outside, he still acted as if he expected to see something.

The nervousness radiating from the boy gave

Maddy anxiety. By the time the end of the day came, it felt as if every one of her nerves stood on edge. "I'm taking you home, Danny."

His eyes widened. "Am I in trouble?"

"I just need to speak with your uncle. You did have a difficult day, didn't you?" She grabbed her backpack. "Maybe your uncle and I can help you deal with whatever is bothering you."

He didn't look convinced and glared at another student who started chanting that Danny was going to get it when he got home. Soon, others joined in, "Danny's gonna get it, Danny's gonna get it."

"That's enough." Maddy clapped her hands. "Hurry on now. See you all tomorrow." Still laughing, the students filed out. Maddy put her hand on Danny's shoulder. "Chin up. It's tough being the new kid. They'll come around soon enough."

"Not if I keep hanging around with the teacher." He lumbered to the parking lot.

"If you'd behave, you wouldn't have to hang out with me." Maddy opened the car door for him.

"I'm talking about you taking me home. It makes me look like teacher's pet." He climbed in and clicked on his seatbelt.

Maybe her taking him home wasn't such a good idea. Still, she knew Ryan would want to get to the bottom of this "monster," and Danny would be more willing to talk to him at home. Hopefully.

The captain's house sat on a few acres outside of town. A barn, a pond, and horses provided an idyllic backdrop for his sprawling, two-storied home. Behind the house, thick trees led to the base of the mountain.

"Nice place." Maddy cut Danny a quick glance.

"I guess. Uncle Ryan found it online and bought it."

She couldn't help but feel a twinge of envy. One of these days, when she'd resolved the real reason she'd come to Misty Hollow, she'd explore the beautiful area. Maddy shoved open her car door as the captain's car pulled up alongside hers.

~

Ryan gave Danny a stern look, then led the way to the front door. The longer he had Danny, the less qualified he felt to raise his nephew. Acting out at school because of lack of sleep?

"Can I get you anything? Water, tea?"

"Water would be fine," Maddy answered. "Do you want to talk in the living room?"

"Make yourself comfortable. Danny, come help me."

The boy's shoulders sagged as if he expected a beating. Neither Ryan or his brother had ever laid a mean hand on him. Another piece of Ryan's heart broke off to shatter into pieces at his feet. "I'm not going to hit you. I'm only wanting to know ahead of time what your teacher is going to tell me."

Danny raised uncertain eyes. "I think she wants to talk to you about monsters."

That was unexpected. Ryan frowned. "Really?"

He nodded. "I mentioned seeing one."

"Remember the story we read about the boy who called wolf?"

"That's why I didn't tell you." He grabbed a juice box from the fridge and left the kitchen.

Ouch. Ryan fixed two tall glasses of ice water and joined the other two in the living room. He handed one glass to Maddy who sat on the sofa, then lowered himself into the easy chair opposite her.

Maddy took a sip, then set the glass on a coaster on the coffee table. "Danny has been missing sleep because of something he sees outside his bedroom window."

Ryan liked that she didn't mince words. "Every night?" He glanced at his nephew.

"When I close my curtains, I see a monster in the woods." Danny seemed to shrink into himself.

Ryan would start closing the curtains himself at night. "Are you sure you aren't having a nightmare like you used to? I've told you to come wake me when you have one."

"I'm awake."

"Perhaps we can show him there's no monster?" Maddy arched a brow. "You're the captain. You'll know what to look for and can ease Danny's mind."

"Do you want me to check?" He asked his nephew.

He nodded. "Take your gun and don't go when it's dark."

Doubt crept into Ryan's mind. What if Danny really had seen something? But why would the perp hang around the home of a captain if he planned on doing something wrong? "Let's go now." He stood and held out his hand.

Danny slid his smaller one in his, for once not being ashamed at holding hands with his uncle. He'd given up on a list of things when he dropped him off at school. Things he'd been ordered not to do because they were embarrassing. Holding hands was at the top of the list, right under a goodbye kiss or hug. If it took an element of danger to have his nephew not shun his touch…Ryan glanced at Maddy. "You coming?"

"Sure. I'm curious as to what keeps a ten-year-old up at night other than a good book or a scary movie." She smiled. "Maybe it's just raccoons climbing over the fence."

"There isn't a fence." Danny would not be swayed.

She shrugged in Ryan's direction. He appreciated that she wanted to help, but his nephew could latch onto an idea like a rabid coon and not let go.

He led the way out the back door he kept meaning to oil and stared toward the trees from the deck. "Which way?"

Danny pointed east. "It's always that way."

Couldn't be an animal, then. Unless something in that spot attracted them enough to keep them coming to the same spot.

Ryan stepped off the deck and headed across the sprawling lawn toward the trees bordering his property. The three walked in silence, Danny's hand starting to tremble as they got closer to where he'd seen the so-called monster. Ryan gave his hand what he hoped was a reassuring squeeze. "Why don't you stand next to Miss Everton while I look around?"

Danny nodded and stepped to his teacher's side.

Searching the ground, Ryan moved slowly around the area. Very little grass grew under the thick foliage. Autumn leaves covered the ground so thick not even his own footprints were left. He'd almost decided there was nothing to see when his gaze landed on a small mound of dirt under a pine tree. Too big to be the burrow of an animal. Too perfect to have been done by nature. He moved closer and froze.

A hand stuck from the center of the mound as if

caught in a wave. The dirt had been packed around the wrist to hold the hand in place. It had been staged.

"Look away, Danny." Ryan turned to see Maddy holding Danny close to her, his face buried in her chest. "I have to call the office. There's no need for him to be here."

"I told you I saw a monster," Danny mumbled.

"Yes, you did. This is a human monster and not one who preys on little boys." Ryan dialed the office.

"I'll take him to the house." Maddy turned, leaving Ryan to deal with the horror of another dead woman.

"What do you have?" Bundt asked, joining Ryan.

"I'm pretty sure it's our latest missing woman, Carol Ridges. Of course, I haven't dug up the body. I'll leave that to the technicians." He stared at the hand with bright pink nail polish.

"Same perp?"

Ryan shrugged. "Allison had been dumped in the lake. This woman is buried. I don't know what to think right now." If it was the same killer, why dispose of the women differently? Was he playing a game with the sheriff's department? "Where's Sheriff Westbrook?"

"On his way." Bundt hunkered down near the hole, touching the woman's fingers with a gloved hand. "No evidence of her fighting back."

"The killer could have eliminated any signs of self-defense." They hadn't found any on Allison's body either, but the lake could have washed away most of the evidence in that case.

"Do you think we have a serial killer on our hands?" Bundt straightened and stared at the house.

"Too early to tell." Ryan followed his gaze to where Maddy and Danny watched from the safe distance of the deck. The town had a serial killer in its midst. He'd followed Ryan here. Why had the killer left Langley and come to Misty Hollow?

Chapter Four

Maddy glanced at the clock again, then at the window. Night set early in November and already starting to get dark at six p.m. She'd told Ryan that she had to work late, and he'd asked her to watch Danny until he finished his shift. Obviously, the investigation took a lot of his time.

"Can I go to the playground?" Danny gave her an imploring look. "It's boring watching you grade papers."

"It's dark outside."

"There's a light."

"No, go play in the gym. If your uncle hasn't arrived when I finish these, I'll take you to my place. We'll order a pizza."

"Yay." His feet thundered down the hall he wasn't allowed to run down during school hours.

Maddy smiled as the door closed with a clang and returned to her work. As the time dragged on and she grew thirsty, she headed to the teacher's lounge for a bottle of water. Another glance at the clock, then she pulled her phone from her pocket and sent Ryan a text saying she'd take Danny home with her.

Ten minutes, he replied.

Wonderful. She hurried back toward her room.

Danny's screams from outside froze her in her tracks, then she burst into a run. As she reached the outside door, a masked man in a dark hoodie slipped inside. He held a knife in his right hand. His eyes glittered as they focused on her.

Fight or flight? The fact Danny's fear-filled yell still sounded outside let her know he hadn't been harmed too much. She whirled and raced toward her room in hopes of locking the door before the man attacked.

Her heart pounded as she turned the knob. Before she could get inside, the man shoved her in and followed.

Danny's screams had stopped. Maddy shot a quick glance at the window, praying the child was okay. She spun around and knocked over desks to slow him down and picked up a chair to use as a shield. "Get out or I'll bash this over your head."

The man advanced, shoving away anything she put between them.

She was going to die like Allison. Throat cut and her body tossed away like garbage. No. She wouldn't. Not today.

She swung the chair with all her might.

The man blocked it with his left hand and yanked it from her grasp. "I like it when they fight." His deep, raspy voice sent ice down her spine.

"Did my sister fight you? I hope she caused pain." Maddy toppled over a bookcase, then bolted through the door he'd left open. She turned from heading to the door he'd entered through and sprinted for the one at the other end of the hall.

Pounding footsteps alerted her that he gave chase.

The door in front of her banged open.

Maddy screamed.

"Get down!" Ryan raised his gun.

Maddy dropped to the floor.

Her assailant slipped into the front office. Glass shattered.

By the time Maddy caught up to Ryan, the man had escaped through the front office window.

Ryan faced her. "Are you okay?"

She nodded. "Danny?"

"In the car. I heard him screaming. He told me he'd seen the monster climb over the fence and enter the building."

Her legs gave way.

Ryan caught her before she fell and lowered her into a chair. "You're okay, Maddy. I got here in time." He knelt in front of her and took her hands in his. "I can't leave Danny too long, and I need to call the sheriff."

"I know," she whispered. "I'll be okay now." She wouldn't ever be okay. Not as long as that man kept killing.

Ryan cupped her cheek, then hurried outside.

Maddy kept her gaze glued to the door, releasing her breath when he came back in with Danny. The child ran into her arms. "You saved me, Danny." She hugged him tight.

"I did?"

"Your cries for help alerted your uncle. He came just in time." She patted his shuddering back, meeting Ryan's worried gaze as he spoke to someone on the phone.

When Ryan hung up, he stood in front of her. "Are you up to showing me where the attack took place? I'd like to take a look before the principal and the sheriff arrive."

"My classroom." Maddy released Danny and got to her feet. She fought the tremors threatening to overwhelm her as she reached her room. With school tomorrow, she'd have to conquer her fear in order to do her job. She hovered in the doorway as Ryan stepped inside.

"Looks like you put up a good fight." He glanced back.

"I did my best." Not that she would have won. Not if Ryan hadn't arrived. Instead of standing over desks she'd knocked over, he'd have been standing over her body.

"Miss Everton?" The principal, Mr. White, approached her with long strides. "Tell me you're okay."

"I'm fine."

He paled after glancing in her room. "I'll have someone set this to rights."

"It's a crime scene, sir. Miss Everton will need another room for a while." Ryan stepped into the hall as Sheriff Westbrook arrived.

"But all my things are in there. My purse and laptop." Maddy shook her head. "I have to go in."

"You may get your personal items," the sheriff said. "But nothing else, I'm afraid."

"I believe you should take some time off until after fall break. It's only a week." Mr. White put a hand on her arm. "I'll get a sub for your students. Miss Snodgrass can make copies of her lessons. That way, you won't be bombarded with questions when the news gets out."

"Okay." That would give Maddy time to settle her nerves. She still couldn't enter the room.

Ryan must have seen her hesitation. "I'll grab your things."

"Thank you. The laptop is on the desk, and my purse is in the right bottom drawer."

~

If Captain Maxwell hadn't arrived, if that stupid kid hadn't started screaming, he'd have the woman he really wanted. Now, he'd have to find a substitute.

He tossed the knife in the passenger seat of his car and squealed tires from the parking lot of the drugstore. The evening had definitely not gone the way he'd planned. Madison should be unconscious in his backseat on the way to where she'd fall in love with him. He'd failed with her sister, but this time he knew Madison was the one.

Now, she'd be wary, always looking over her shoulder. Skittish like an abused horse.

He cursed and pounded the steering wheel. Deep breaths. You need to think clearly. You need to find the next woman. The night doesn't have to be a complete waste.

He removed his mask and hoodie, tossing them both in the seat with the gun. Now that he was thinking clearly, he knew where to go. The VFW hall had bingo that night. It always attracted both young and old women. There should be at least one lovely blonde in attendance.

Turned out there were two. He watched from the safety of his car as they stepped outside for some fresh air. He decided on the one with the longest hair and settled back to wait until he could follow his choice home.

~

When Ryan had heard Danny's screams, then his shouting that the monster went in the school, he wasn't sure what to expect. Definitely not the sight of a masked man with a knife in his hand after Maddy. Now, Ryan crossed the classroom that looked as if a tornado had hit it and collected Maddy's things. He was glad the principal told her to take a few days off. Maddy definitely looked to be in a state of shock and nowhere near ready to enter this room.

Ryan collected the items she'd requested and handed them to her. He needed to ask her to take Danny home with her while he processed the scene but knew he couldn't. She wasn't ready to be alone. Instead, he asked her to stay and insisted she go home with him.

"Why can't you call in Deputy Bundt?" Her forehead creased.

"He's not on duty tonight. You'll be staying in my guestroom for a while, too."

"No." She shook her head. "I'll be fine in my house."

"Allison was taken from that house." He regretted his words the instant he'd spoken them.

Her features fell. "I can't live in fear."

"You should. At least until this guy is caught." He crossed his arms and set his features into the impassive face he called his cop mask.

Danny slipped his hand into Maddy's. "Please? I don't want that man to get you."

"You realize it isn't a monster?" She smiled down

at him.

Nodding, Danny said, "Just a really bad man."

A real-life monster. Ryan asked Mr. White to take Maddy and Danny somewhere they could relax until he finished there.

"You think it's the same man who's been killing our women?" Sheriff Westbrook asked.

"I do. Sir, I think we may have a serial killer on our hands."

"In Misty Hollow?" He frowned. "The selection is pretty small here. We've had our share of trouble, but a serial killer sounds a bit far-fetched."

How could a former FBI agent not see what Ryan saw? He knew of the sheriff's record. Knew he'd married the daughter of a crime lord after helping her put her father behind bars. "I think we should call in the FBI."

"Not yet. I'm not fully convinced. Besides, we do that, and we'll have the town in a panic. We're getting close, Captain. You almost had him tonight."

"Miss Everton was almost taken. My nephew is a witness." He fought to keep his voice from rising. "Sir, I followed this killer from Langley. He'd killed four women there. He's definitely a serial."

"All right, I'll consider your suggestion. I'll call a buddy of mine and see what he thinks."

It was something. From the worry on the sheriff's face, he did believe the way Ryan did. Why the reluctance to call for help? Was it really to keep the town from panicking?

Several hours later, Ryan went looking for Maddy and his nephew. Both slept on beds in the nurse's office. He stood between them, his eyes darting from one face to the other. He could have lost one or both of them tonight.

No one had ever escaped this killer. Maddy would have been taken, only to resurface in three days, her body dumped somewhere for an unsuspecting person to find. He couldn't let that happen. His heart and his nephew would never recover.

"Take them home, Captain. Your night isn't over yet." The sheriff stood behind him. "I need you to meet me at the VFW. We've got another missing woman."

His heart dropped the same time Maddy's eyes popped open. "If he'd taken me, that woman would have been safe," she whispered.

"You don't know that. He would have taken her in three days." Ryan scooped Danny into his arms. "Let's get the two of you settled. My house has an alarm. No one can get in." Still, although he had one of the safest houses in town, he hated having to leave them. Nothing was safer than he was, armed and waiting for the killer to come.

"I'll need some things from my place," Maddy said, sliding into the front passenger seat.

"We'll stop by there." He sat Danny in the backseat and buckled him in. The boy's head bobbed, but he didn't wake up.

Ryan climbed behind the wheel and glanced at Maddy. "I'm sorry this is happening. I know you came to seek answers about your sister's death, not expecting to become a target yourself."

"This town should be a safe haven. Something this beautiful shouldn't harbor evil. Misty Mountain looks as if it should cover the town, protecting it like a hen does its chicks." She faced him. "Now, it looks like a shadow ready to engulf everything."

He wanted to tell her that Misty Hollow was all she'd thought, but he hadn't lived here long enough to know. Maybe the town wasn't only a place where those looking for small-town life could come, but also a town where evil hid.

Chapter Five

For three days Maddie stayed in Ryan's guestroom. How much longer?

She sniffed. Coffee. Just what she needed. She threw aside the quilt she'd covered up with. The flannel pajama bottoms and tee shirt she slept in were modest enough she could leave her room without a robe.

"Good morning." She tousled Danny's hair as he sat at the kitchen island. "I see you're a big help to your uncle."

"I'm not doing anything." He frowned.

She laughed. "That's my point."

"Good morning." Ryan folded an omelet in a pan on the stove. "It's Danny's job to set the table." He narrowed his eyes. "Right? Before I'm finished cooking?"

"Yes." The boy rolled his eyes. "I don't like my teacher living here. She's making me work, even though we aren't at school."

"It's almost fall break." Maddy laughed and poured herself a cup of coffee. "No homework, then."

"Yay." He scooted off the stool and grabbed three plates from the dish drainer by the sink.

"Can I help with anything?" Maddy added creamer

to her coffee.

"No, I've got it. Thanks. What are your plans for today?"

"Some research and assigning schoolwork for Danny." She laughed as the boy's scowl deepened.

"Good. I'd like to head to work and help with the investigation. I can't catch the guy if I stay at home." He placed the last omelet on a plate with two others and carried them to the table.

Hopefully, her research would dig up something to help him. "I'd like to return home."

"I don't think that's wise. Aren't you comfortable here?"

"Very, but Thanksgiving is…"

"So? Celebrate with me and Danny." He lowered his voice. "It'll be the first one without his parents. You might help provide a distraction for him."

She doubted anything would erase the boy's grief but nodded. "Okay. I'll leave after then."

"Maybe we'll catch this guy."

She hoped so. Returning to her sister's place with a killer roaming the town might not be the smartest thing, but she hated imposing. Watching Danny while Ryan went to work each day helped ease her guilt for being there. "Maybe I should install a security system where I'm living."

"You plan on staying in Misty Hollow?"

"At least through the schoolyear." She'd signed a contract. "Who knows after that." She had no ties anywhere else. Maddy ate quickly and showered so she'd be dressed and ready for the day before Ryan had to leave. When she'd finished, she carried her laptop to the kitchen table where she'd do research while Danny completed the day's schoolwork.

"See you later. Be good." Ryan gave Danny a one-armed hug. "How about I bring home Chinese food tonight?" His gaze landed on Maddy.

"Sounds good to me." She sat and opened her laptop. "Danny, you have an hour before school starts."

He raced for the living room. Seconds later, sounds of an animated show drifted from the room.

Maddy went to a national news site and typed in, *blondes missing for three days before their bodies found.* Allison hadn't been the first. A woman had been found in Langley, a Rachel Schultz. The woman found in the woods behind Ryan's house made the third victim, that Maddy could easily find anyway. But, another woman had gone missing last night. Would she be number four?

Sighing, she continued searching. She could've been number four herself. Finding a clue to the identity of whom the newspapers were calling "The Abductor" could very well protect her and the other women of Misty Hollow.

It would be a miracle if she found a clue the authorities had missed. But, she had to do something to keep her mind busy, or she'd go insane.

"Danny. Math time." She slid several pages of math problems across the table. She thought it best to start the day with the subject he enjoyed the most.

With only one student, the day's work was finished by lunchtime. Ham and cheese sandwich on a plate next to her laptop, Maddy continued her online search. The further she dug, the more deaths she found that resembled the latest. The first ones were in Langley.

"This looks like we have a serial killer. One that

has moved from Langley to Misty Hollow," she whispered. She glanced at the open curtains over the kitchen window.

The killer had been watching Ryan's house…buried a woman out back. Why? What kind of a game was The Abductor playing?

~

Ryan had asked questions of everyone at the Bingo hall the night before. No one had seen anything. Not even the missing woman's friend. She said her friend had gone outside for some fresh air with her and stayed out a little longer. No one had seen her since. Vanished, just like the women in the past.

"Sheriff Westbrook is reluctant to call in the feds," he told Bundt as they drove back to the station. "I think we have a serial killer on our hands and not enough manpower to find this Abductor. Why does the media insist on nicknames?"

Bundt shrugged. "Makes more sense than simply saying the killer, I guess. How's it going with Miss Everton? The two of you, you know?"

Ryan frowned. "She's nothing more than a guest in my home and a tutor for my nephew who's afraid to return to school right now. It's strictly professional."

"Then it's all right if I ask her out?"

"Be my guest." He didn't care. Then why the niggle of jealousy when the other man expressed his attraction for Maddy? "At least you're a cop and can keep her safe."

"You really think we have a serial killer?" Bundt turned sideways in his seat. "In Misty Hollow?" He shook his head. "That's a big-city thing."

"Not necessarily." His hands tightened on the

steering wheel. "I think it's the same killer that was doing this in Langley not too long ago."

"Got tired of a place with lots of opportunities for one where everyone watches what everyone else is doing? Sounds far-fetched."

"It's happening, isn't it?" Why did everyone seem so hesitant to believe they had a potential serial killer in Misty Hollow? He pulled into the parking lot of the station. Time to type up his report before picking up that evening's supper.

"Don't fret. We'll either catch this guy or he'll move on." Bundt opened his door and exited the car.

True, but how many women would die before that happened? Ryan might have followed the killer to Misty Hollow, but this town was quickly becoming home. Friendly people who appreciated their local law enforcement. Until The Abductor, crime was relatively low, except for last fall's murders. That whole thing should have been an isolated incident. A stalker after one woman, not multiple.

He turned off the car and headed to his desk in the bullpen. A sheriff, a captain, and two deputies were all that made up Misty Hollow law enforcement. They needed help. If the sheriff didn't act soon, Ryan would have to go over his head.

Typing up all the questions and answers from the bingo hall took an hour. He hoped Maddy wouldn't mind a late supper. "See you tomorrow, Bundt. You on duty tonight?"

"Yep. Pulling a double shift." He crossed his ankles on his desk and folded his arms behind his head. "Tomorrow is your turn. Sleep well."

Ryan waved to the sheriff, who didn't look as if

he'd slept in days, as he strolled from the building. He called in an order for Chinese, then stopped at the small restaurant to pick up the order. By the time he got home, seven o'clock had arrived and night had fallen. He shook his head to see every single light on in the house. It would take a long time before Danny would be comfortable without a lot of lights.

Ryan carried the food inside and set the boxes on the kitchen table. Through the doorway, he saw Maddy and Danny watching a sitcom. "Supper's ready."

They both jerked at his voice.

"Sorry. You must not have heard me come in."

"We didn't." Maddy unfolded herself from the sofa. "Smells good. I'm starving."

"I know it's late. Sorry about that." He reached into the cupboard and pulled down three plates. "Danny, come eat."

He huffed and turned off the TV, then came to set the table.

"I need to talk to you later," Maddy said. "In private."

"All right."

"Can I eat in front of the TV?" Danny reached for the box of orange chicken. "I was right in the middle of the show."

Ryan glanced at Maddy. They wouldn't have to wait to talk if Danny was in the other room. "That's fine." After the boy scampered off, Ryan sat and started to fill his plate. "What's up?"

Maddy sat, nibbling on an egg roll. "The research I did today convinced me there is a serial killer in Misty Hollow. The same thing that happened to Allison happened to several women in Langley. Why hasn't the sheriff called in the FBI?"

"That's my question, too." He met her gaze. "One of the women in Langley was my cousin. When I read about your sister, I checked for an opening at the sheriff's department. That's why I came to this town. The same reason you did. To get answers."

~

He had just enough time to give Shelby water and a sandwich. She whimpered and scooted as far away from him as her bindings would allow, the blanket he'd provided slipping from her shoulders. "Don't be frightened. It's very simple. All I want is your love." He set the things down where she'd be able to reach, then stepped back. "It's really that simple. Love me, and everything will be fine."

"You're The Abductor." Tears welled in her eyes. "How could I love someone like you?"

Heat rose up his neck and onto his face. "I hate that name." He spun around and left, slamming the door behind him. She'd be like all the rest. It was Maddy he needed. None of the others would work. Still, he had to keep trying until he got close enough to Maddy. He couldn't give up hope.

He marched down the hall, ignoring the screams coming from the room that held Shelby. Let her make all the noise she wanted. No one would hear her. Not on five acres of land. That's why he'd bought the place. For the privacy.

The further he moved from the room, the happier he grew. He never could stay angry at one of his girls for long.

He poured himself some whiskey over ice and settled into his easy chair that overlooked the sprawling lawn he kept mowed. Of course, now that it was fall, the grass had turned brown, but the trees sported their autumn foliage. He'd never grow tired of the view out his front window. The only thing missing was a beautiful blonde enjoying the view with him.

With a sigh, he took a sip of his drink. He felt invincible. The sheriff's department was incompetent. It was easy to stay one step ahead of them. Let them run around trying to catch him. They'd fail, always. Just like the Langley police department.

Time to return to work. He'd been gone too long as it was. After draining his glass, he drove back to Misty Hollow. He slowed in front of the captain's house hoping to catch a glimpse of Maddy. There. Sitting at the kitchen table with a serious look on her face.

He wanted to erase the worry there. Surely, she'd smile when she fell in love with him. She had to. If not, she'd suffer the same fate as the others, and he'd keep looking.

Chapter Six

Maddy couldn't believe she'd agreed to go on a date with Deputy Bundt. What happened to no time for a relationship? Now, she stood in front of her mirror fixing her hair wishing she was watching a holiday movie with Danny and Ryan.

"Date's here." Ryan leaned against the door frame. "Explain to me why you're going out with the deputy?"

"A moment of weakness." She shrugged. "It's only dinner. I won't be late."

"You should be safe enough with Bundt. Have a good time." He strode away.

If Maddy didn't know any better, she'd think Ryan might be a bit jealous. The thought put a little more spring in her step, which elicited a wide smile from her date. "Hello, Lance."

"You look nice, Maddy. All eyes will be on us tonight." He handed her a bouquet of pink roses.

"I'll put these in water for you." Ryan snatched them from the deputy. "Be careful."

Lance's eyes flashed, but his smile remained. "Shall we?"

"Of course." Maddy narrowed her eyes at Ryan, then let Lance escort her to his navy SUV.

"I hope you like seafood. There's a great place in Langley."

"I do." She reached for her seatbelt only to have Lance lean over and click it for her. Her stomach tightened. He took his time straightening back up, his breath warm on her cheek. Instead of feeling romantic, she squirmed, scooting as close to the door as possible. It was going to be a long couple of hours.

Lance did most of the talking on the half-hour drive, telling her how he was the third generation to go into law enforcement. That he'd chosen Misty Hollow for the small-town vibe and not having to worry when going out in uniform that someone would shoot him.

Maddy responded when she needed to and let him ramble on. When he pulled into the restaurant parking lot, she couldn't climb out of the car fast enough.

"A gentleman always opens the door for a lady." Lance frowned as he rushed around the front of the car.

"Oh, I'm sorry. I'm used to doing things on my own." Maddy stiffened when he placed his hand on the small of her back. Why did she act so prudish? Because she hadn't been on a date for almost a year. She forced herself to relax.

"You smell nice." Lance leaned over and took a whiff of her neck.

"Thank you." She frowned. The man didn't act as if they were on their first date. More like their tenth.

A hostess in black slacks, white blouse, and black tie led them to a booth, placing menus on the table. "Robert will be your server."

Lance took the menu and handed them to the hostess. "We'll both have the filet and shrimp. Medium rare. Blue cheese crust. Ranch dressing on the salads.

Please let our server know. Oh, a bottle of your finest wine."

Maddy started to protest his ordering for her but stopped. She probably would've ordered the same thing. "Just ice water for me."

"You won't have a glass of wine with me?" Lance looked hurt. "We're celebrating what promises to be a wonderful relationship."

Was this man serious? After thirty minutes in her company and he thought they were in a relationship? "Lance, I prefer to take things slow. Let's be friends first, okay? I'm here to find out answers about my sister, not for romance."

His eyes flashed again. Ah, his tell when angered. Still, the smile remained. "We'll do things your way." He reached over and placed his hand on hers.

She coughed and reached for her napkin evading his grasp before folding her hands in her lap. Their server, a young man with a nametag that read Robert, brought their salads.

"You guys must be in a hurry. I've never had anyone give the order to the hostess before. Is there anything else I can bring you? Your entrees should be ready soon."

"Thank you." Maddy glanced up, acknowledging the server.

"What are you doing for Thanksgiving?" Lance tried to reach for her hand again when she moved for her water glass.

Again she dodged his grasp and kept her hands in her lap. Hopefully, when the steak arrived, Lance would be too busy eating to try holding her hand. "I've accepted an invitation from the captain to spend the day with him and Danny. It's the first holiday since Danny's parents died, and we thought it would help lessen the pain."

His gaze hardened. "I guess I can understand that."

She almost invited him until realizing it wasn't her place. Ryan and the deputy didn't seem to be the best of friends anyway. Still, although uncomfortable about Lance's intense attention, she didn't like anyone to spend the holidays alone.

Their meal arrived and conversation turned to the abductions. "I heard someone came into the school after you." Lance cut his steak.

"Yes. If not for Danny's screams, Ryan might not have come inside."

"You must have been frightened."

"Very much."

"You're safe with me. You realize that, don't you?"

"Yes." She bit into the steak. "Delicious. I've actually considered dying my hair."

"Absolutely not."

"Excuse me?" She widened her eyes.

"I mean, you shouldn't. Everyone already knows the color of your hair. You won't be fooling this guy."

True, but he had no right to tell her not to color her hair. When she'd finished as much as she could eat, she set her fork on the plate, relieved that this date was coming to an end. Would faking a headache end the date early?

"It's a nice night. How about a walk around the pond outside?"

She studied his face. Drat, she'd have to take the walk.

A slight chill kissed the autumn night. Maddy pulled her leather coat tight, keeping her hands out of Lance's reach.

The man would not be deterred. He zipped up her coat, then took her right hand in his as if they really were a romantic couple out for a stroll.

The night wouldn't end fast enough.

~

Headlights through the front window alerted Ryan that Maddy was home. He almost rose to his feet to see if she let Bundt kiss her goodnight. It was none of his business. Ryan grabbed a magazine and did his best to appear nonchalant.

The front door opened, and Maddy stepped inside, leaning against it. She heaved a heavy sigh.

"Fun night?"

She jerked to face him. "Not particularly." Maddy unzipped her coat and shrugged out of it before Ryan could help. She hung it on a hook near the door and toed off her black heels. "Who asks a girl to go for a walk when she's wearing heels?"

"You could have told him you weren't wearing the proper shoes. Want coffee?"

"That sounds wonderful. Decaf?"

"Got it." He'd already made a pot in case she wanted to settle down before going to bed. He poured them both a cup, then returned to the living room. "Want to talk about it?"

"Why are you so curious?" She narrowed her eyes over the rim.

"I'm new to town. I'd like to know what people here do on dates."

"You're just being nosy." She smiled.

He laughed. "Guilty."

She crossed her ankles on the coffee table, giving him a good look at her shapely calves. "I don't think I'll go out with him again. He's…forceful."

"What?" Ryan stiffened.

"Just touchy, and he practically forbade me to color my hair."

"Your hair?"

"Just an idea until The Abductor is captured. Of course, Lance had a point. In this small town, I wouldn't be fooling anyone. Add to that the deputy acted possessive and seemed to think we were in a relationship. Well, the evening was a bit uncomfortable. I'm going to stick to my resolve not to get involved until I've accomplished what I came for."

"The killer." Her determination could very well get her murdered.

"Yes. He's going to mess up at some point."

"Maddy, you aren't law enforcement. You need to stay safe and let us do our jobs."

She tilted her head, determination etched on her face. "Isn't that why I'm here? To be kept safe? School resumes next Monday. I intend on doing *my* job. When I'm not, I'll keep searching for the identity of the person who killed my sister. Any bodies discovered today?" She asked.

"No, why?"

"This is the third day after the girl was taken from bingo."

He glanced at the clock on the wall. Ten p.m. There was still time. He called the sheriff to confirm no bodies had been found.

"Not yet," the sheriff replied. "I'm patrolling the

streets tonight until Bundt takes the late shift. It's quiet."

Ryan pushed the off button. His nerves hummed. The killer hadn't missed the third day since he'd started killing. He glanced at the clock again.

Danny screamed.

"Stay there." He pointed to Maddy, then thundered up the stairs and into his nephew's room.

Danny stood by the window. "He's out there."

"Who is out there?"

"The bad guy."

Ryan peered out. He couldn't see anything moving. "Are you sure?"

"He stepped out of the trees, then jumped back when I screamed. I saw him. I promise." Fear riddled his face.

"Go downstairs to Miss Everton. I'll be right back. Tell her to call the sheriff." Retrieving his gun and a flashlight from his room, Ryan raced out the back door and toward the direction Danny had spotted something.

It didn't take long for the cold to seep through his tee-shirt and the slippers on his feet. Come on. Show yourself.

Ryan clicked on the flashlight and moved it back and forth trying to find a sign. There. Footprints, wide-spaced, like the person was running. He tried to figure out if he could recognize the pattern of the print.

A twig snapped off to his left. He turned off the flashlight and listened.

The rustling of leaves.

A dull thump.

At a crouch, Ryan moved quietly in that direction. He hadn't gone more than fifty yards before stumbling, literally, over a body still warm. Ryan knelt and felt for a pulse. Nothing. The killer had dumped his latest victim mere seconds before he stumbled across her.

Ryan studied the area around him. Leaves carpeted the ground too heavily for more prints to be left behind. Pounding feet came his way. He lifted his gun.

"Whoa." The sheriff came into view. "Miss Everton told me what Danny saw." He glanced at the body. "This is the second one on your property."

"He's taunting me." Ryan lowered his weapon. "The killer's toying with us. He'll slip up, and we'll get him. Almost had him tonight."

"Hope it's soon."

~

That was a blast. Close, but he still roamed the streets a free man. The captain had been right on his heels. The fact he hadn't been caught was a testament to his intelligence. He'd continue to outsmart them until he finished what he'd come for.

What had the boy been doing up so late? If he hadn't seen him, he might have been able to get close enough to lay eyes on the one he wanted. The boy was quickly becoming a nuisance.

No matter. He had another woman to find either tonight or tomorrow. Of course, he didn't want too much time to pass. Had to keep the momentum going. The time for Maddy would come. Until then, he'd have his fun.

It wasn't as if he could stop. No, the desire to kill consumed him. A constant hunger. Even when he found the woman to love him, he knew he'd continue to kill. The only difference would be that there'd be a beautiful woman waiting for him when he came home.

Something he'd dreamed of forever. Something that had been taken away from him when Sarah chose death over a life with him. He'd find her replacement. He knew it.

Chapter Seven

Susan entered Maddy's classroom at the end of the day, the first Monday after Thanksgiving. "I'm leaving town for a while. I suggest you do the same. Especially since you've already been targeted."

"What do you mean?" She glanced up from grading papers.

"Another blonde went missing last night." She lifted her honey-colored hair. "I'm not taking any chances, and I'm not the only one. Others at the diner were saying the same thing. Women are fleeing this place until The Abductor is caught."

Tempting, but Maddy refused to run in fear. She wanted to be around when the man was caught. Wanted to stare into his eyes so he could see how much she hated him. "I'm staying."

"Hopefully, I'll see you again and not your face on the news report." Susan left.

There was one other blond teacher at the school, a middle-aged woman. Since The Abductor preferred them on the younger side, she should be safe. No one over the age of thirty had disappeared or been found dead.

She set the pile of schoolwork on the corner of her

desk and collected her backpack. Ryan hadn't been happy that morning when she'd told him she had some work to do after school and would drive herself and Danny home.

She found him in another classroom with the son of one of the sixth-grade teachers. "Ready?"

"Yep." He jumped to his feet, grabbed his backpack, and raced from the room. "Ice cream?"

"Don't you think it's too close to supper? Your uncle said he'd be home in time to eat with us. I thought maybe we could make spaghetti. You can slather garlic butter on the bread."

"Okay." He shrugged. "Jack told me that Miss Snodgrass is leaving town for a while."

"I also heard that." She pressed the bar to open the outside door and a chilly gust of air blasted her in the face. "It gets cold in the mountains, doesn't it?" Living in the valley hadn't prepared her for such a temperature change.

"I can't wait until it snows." Danny climbed in the backseat of her car.

"Seatbelt." Maddy slid into the driver's seat and turned on the car, then the heater. Hopefully, it wouldn't take long to warm up.

Maddy pulled from her parking space and away from the school. Ryan and Danny only lived a couple of blocks from the school, but as frigid as the morning had been, Maddy hadn't wanted to walk. She glanced in her rearview mirror to see another car pull out behind her.

Whoever it was followed too close. Maddy increased her speed just a bit. They did, too. She'd have a talk tomorrow with whoever owned the vehicle.

She turned a corner, and the car followed. Were

they following her? Rather than go home, she turned in the opposite direction. So did the other car. Another turn and then another.

"Where are we going?" Danny asked. "This isn't the way to the house."

"We're going to go say hey to your uncle." Wasn't that what a person should do if they suspected they were being followed? Go to the local police station?

She parked as close to the building as possible. The other car pulled into the parking lot entrance and idled there.

"Come on." She rushed Danny from the car and into the building.

Ryan turned from the receptionist desk as the door banged open. "Hey, you two."

Maddy handed Danny a dollar bill. "Go get yourself something from the vending machine." When he'd left, she turned to Ryan. "Someone followed us from school. They were still in the parking lot when we came in here. Dark sedan. Dark blue, green, or black. I'm not sure."

"Stay here." Ryan dashed outside.

Maddy peered through the glass in the door. Ryan stood in front of the building and glanced this way and that. The car wasn't where it had been. No doubt, the driver had left once she took Danny inside.

Ryan came back in. "I won't be home as early as I'd thought. The sheriff has called in the FBI, and since I'm the lead on this case—"

"They aren't coming now until morning." Sheriff Westbrook joined them.

Ryan filled him in on why Maddy and Danny were there.

The sheriff nodded. "Follow them home. I'll see you in the morning."

Some of the tension drained from Maddy. "Thank you, Sheriff."

"Be safe, Miss Everton."

"I'll be right behind you." Ryan smiled over her shoulder at Danny. "Chips, huh? Hope it doesn't ruin your supper."

"It won't. We're having spaghetti."

Maddy laughed. "Then, we'd best get moving." She constantly checked her rearview mirror on the way to Ryan's house, reassuring herself that he stayed behind her. How was she supposed to go to and from work? She guessed she could ride the school bus, although Danny refused to so far. Having a teacher on the bus wouldn't go over well with the students.

Walking was out of the question. If the person who'd followed them had ill intentions, which she suspected, they'd be easy targets walking. This abductor person kept Maddy too busy to dig into her sister's death. She needed to find a way to stop him.

~

"Women are leaving town?" Agent Starling widened her eyes.

"Yes. Several blondes are already gone." Ryan twirled a pencil between his fingers. "My son's teacher is staying with me because there was already an attempt to abduct her. Her sister was killed last month. Yesterday, someone followed her and my nephew from the school." He dropped the pencil and folded his hands on the table. "So, what's the plan? There'll be another body tomorrow or the next day. Two of which have been dropped on my property."

"Why is that, Captain Maxwell?" Agent Reed asked. "Why you?"

"That's the million-dollar question."

"Maybe this perp has a vendetta against you." Bundt arched a brow. "Made any enemies since you arrived?"

Just him. "No. I've been too busy with this case to do much of anything else."

"We'd like to see where the bodies were dropped on your property, Captain," Agent Lee said.

Ryan stood. "We can go now. I'd rather do this while my nephew isn't home. It's been traumatizing for him."

"I understand. Sheriff?"

"Bundt and I will stay here in case we receive a call about another body. Agents, we have no clues regarding this person. Nothing more than he sticks religiously to a schedule. I have the feeling we won't know who he is unless we catch him in the act. The body count is rising with no end in sight."

Depressing, but a true statement. Ryan followed the agents outside and into their SUV. The only words spoken on the drive were the directions Ryan gave.

"All I've found at either site is one footprint." Ryan led the way to the first place. "The body had been partially buried with dirt and leaves. The second body was on the other side of the lawn and still warm. I also believe the man killing women in Misty Hollow started in Langley."

"We believe he started in Morrison last year." Agent Lee hunkered next to where Ryan had found the first body. "He's elusive and skilled. Knows what he's doing and stays one step ahead of us. The sheriff should have called us sooner."

"In his defense, he'd hoped we didn't have a serial killer on our hands." Ryan crossed his arms and leaned against a tree.

"Show us the second site, Captain."

Ryan led them across the yard. "My nephew spotted the man from his bedroom window."

"He was approaching the house?" Lee exchanged a glance with Starling.

"It appears that way. Until Danny started screaming and I ran after the guy. He had too much of a head start for me to catch him. We've had a mold made of the footprint." He showed him where the perp's foot had landed in damp dirt.

"Why would he approach the house of law enforcement?" Starling frowned. "That's pretty bold."

"To catch a glimpse of the one that got away. Madison Everton." Ryan swallowed past a sudden dry throat. It hadn't occurred to him until that moment that she could be the reason the person had stepped into the open.

He turned toward the house. Danny's window had a clear view of this side of the yard. Below that was the living room where the curtains were usually open. Living outside of town, Ryan hadn't felt the need to close the house up like a prison at night. That would all change now.

"Which way did the person run?"

"To the south."

The agents marched in that direction. Ryan followed them to an old logging road that bordered his property.

"He must've had a vehicle waiting here." Starling

studied tire tracks.

"No one ever uses this road," Ryan said.

"Then whoever we're looking for is familiar with the area."

"He could find what he needed from Google. An aerial view would show this road clear enough." Ryan stepped into the road.

He'd never gone in either direction to see where the road led or if there were other houses. Across from him was government land where several of the locals hunted during deer season. "What if there's a hunting cabin close by? He could be staying there."

"We'll have the area searched. Thank you for your help, but we'll take the case from here."

"You don't think you need my help?"

"We'll ask you if we do." Lee strode back to the SUV.

Ryan had thought they'd work with him not take over. How could he keep Maddy safe if he wasn't kept up to speed on the investigation?

~

The feds didn't have any better chance of catching him than Maxwell or the sheriff. He moved among them, strolled the sidewalks, and no one gave him a second glance.

He rolled his latest victim in plastic, then hefted her over his shoulder. What a perfect place to lay this one to rest. This late at night, everyone would be asleep. He put her in the trunk, then climbed into the driver's seat wishing he could see their faces when they discovered her.

After staging her where she'd be found in the morning, he drove home to get some sleep before work tomorrow. *If* he could sleep with all the anticipation coursing through him. He'd have to make time the next day or night to grab the next one. All this work made him tired.

He fished an energy drink from the small cooler he kept on the passenger seat and popped the tab. Now, he'd certainly not fall asleep right away. Well, he'd stay up for a while and make plans.

Maddy had been smart pulling into the sheriff's office. That's why she'd be perfect when the time came. Smart and beautiful. The boy, though…he'd have to be disposed of since the lovely teacher rarely went anywhere without him.

When the time came, his plan had to be flawless. Of course, he had no plans to Maddy. He couldn't be that wrong about her, could he?

He drummed his fingers on the steering wheel. She stayed at Maxwell's house, but he was fairly certain they weren't sharing a room. Strictly a platonic relationship. He hoped.

If not, then she would receive the same fate as the others.

Chapter Eight

Maddy grabbed her backpack. "Danny, we're going to be late." She had an early staff meeting at that school she couldn't miss.

"I can drop him off at school." Ryan, bare-chested and wearing flannel pajama bottoms, entered the kitchen drying his hair with a towel.

Swallowing against the sudden lump in her throat, Maddy yanked her gaze from his torso and reached for the front door handle. "Thanks." She stepped outside, pulling the door closed behind her.

Her pack flew from her hands as she landed hard on her hands and knees. Her eyes landed on the blank stare of a dead woman. Maddy screamed and scuttled back.

Seconds later, Ryan barged outside, took one look at the woman, and ordered Danny to stay inside. "You okay?" He helped her to her feet.

"I think so. He's been on the porch. While we were sleeping." Her hands and legs trembled bad enough she had to sit in a chair. If this man can get this close, he might be able to access the house. Sneak up the stairs. Kill her.

"Call the sheriff." Ryan knelt and felt for a pulse.

Maddy quickly dialed 911 and reported a dead woman on Captain Maxwell's porch. It looked like she'd be missing her morning staff meeting, so she placed a call to the school for them to call in a substitute teacher. She didn't have any idea when she'd be back to work.

"I need to get dressed and be ready when the sheriff arrives. Keep an eye on...her...from the window, okay?" Ryan straightened and surveyed the area. "The perp might be watching."

Maddy climbed shakily to her feet and scanned the area. Her skin crawled. "Okay." She turned for the door and caught sight of Danny peering through the window. From the wide-eyed look on his face, she guessed he'd caught a glimpse of the woman.

Inside, she waved him away from the window. "There are some things a child shouldn't see." She took up where he'd been standing as Ryan entered and headed upstairs.

The poor woman's body, discarded as if she had no value. What kind of person would taunt the captain by dumping the body here?

Maddy wrapped her arms around herself. This place no longer felt safe.

The sheriff and Lance arrived together.

Ryan rushed down the stairs and out the door. He came to a sudden halt when he reached her. "Your knees are bleeding."

"Oh." She hadn't felt the scrapes. Now that she knew about her knees, they burned like the dickens.

In the downstairs bathroom, she scrubbed her knees with a cloth wet with hot water and hissed against the pain. Then she sprayed, spread cream, and attached

Band-aids before going to her room to change her pants.

Danny was watching a cartoon when she returned to the living room.

Maddy put a hand on his shoulder. "You okay?"

"Yep," his response barely rose above a whisper.

"Your uncle will catch this guy."

"I know."

She glanced out the window to see two people in dark suits. The FBI agents? The female agent caught Maddy looking and waved for her to come outside.

"I'll be right outside if you need me." Her heart ached at all Danny had gone through in the last six months. No child should see so much death.

"Since there's very little blood, I'd say her throat was slit somewhere else and she was moved here," the male agent said.

"Maddy, these are Special Agents Starling and Lee. They've taken over the investigation." From the curt way Ryan spoke, he wasn't happy about the situation.

"You found the body, Miss Everton?" Agent Starling arched a thin eyebrow.

"I tripped over it...her as I was leaving to go to work."

"You didn't see anything?" Agent Lee asked.

"We were all sleeping."

Lance moved to her side, standing so close to her his arm brushed hers. "An awful thing to see first thing. Bad way to start the day."

That was an understatement. She crossed her arms and took a step away from him. "Not a good way, that's for sure."

"I'm here if you need me." His gaze roamed her face. "I'd like to take you out again. How about Saturday?"

"I'll get back to you."

He curled his lip and went to stand next to the sheriff. His gaze remained on her rather than the woman at their feet.

An ambulance pulled behind the sheriff's jeep. Two paramedics climbed out, then rolled a stretcher toward the porch.

"I'm certain this is the latest missing girl," Sheriff Westbrook said, "but I'll notify her family to send someone to positively identify." He turned to Ryan. "Captain, there are too many ways for a person to get close to this house. The trees provide the perfect hiding place. I suggest the three of you move to Miss Everton's. A house in town will be harder for someone to get close to."

"I have an excellent security system here." Ryan scowled.

The sheriff nodded. "I suggest Miss Everton install one at her house. Also, cameras. You need as much warning as you can get."

Maddy glanced from the sheriff's face to Ryan's. He didn't look pleased about being asked to relocate. She didn't blame him. This house had a lot more room. But, she agreed with the sheriff. Being in town meant more eyes on them, nosy neighbors, folks looking out for each other. Plus, it was closer to the sheriff's office and help if they needed it.

And, she knew they'd need the help. The killer wouldn't stop.

~

Ryan did not like the idea of uprooting Danny. His nephew had been through enough change in his life. But the hopeful look on Maddy's face had him agreeing to go. "I'll let my nephew know."

"The boy is the only one alive who has seen this person," the sheriff said. "Being in town will be safer for him."

Ryan nodded and entered the house. He sat across from Danny. "Will you turn off the TV and give me your attention, please?"

Danny sighed and pressed the off button on the remote. "Do I have to go to school today?"

"If Miss Everton goes, yes. That isn't what I need to talk to you about." He took a deep breath. "Because this bad guy came so close to this house, the sheriff wants us to go stay in Miss Everton's house for a while. Will you be okay with that?"

"We haven't been here long enough for me to get attached."

"It's still a change."

Danny shrugged. "It's cool."

"You're growing up." Ryan stood. "Go pack your things. If you forget something, we can always come back and get it."

Maddy headed upstairs. Soon all three had packed, the body was removed from the front porch, and Ryan followed Maddy to her place.

Inside the small cottage-style house, he checked all three bedrooms, the one bathroom, and the main living space. "All clear." Ryan set his bag on the bed in the bedroom closest to the front door. He wanted to tell himself it was so he'd hear anyone sneaking past, but he hadn't heard anything when the body was dumped.

Was he losing his touch?

He'd unpack later. Right now, he needed to check the yard. Ryan stepped out the kitchen door. Wooden privacy fence on a postage-stamp-sized yard. Anyone could jump the fence and be at the door in seconds. He called the local hardware store and ordered four cameras to be delivered that day—one for every corner of the house.

"You shouldn't be spending your money on those." Maddy moved up behind him. "I can pay for the cameras."

"Consider it my contribution for Danny and me staying here." He smiled. "Plus, it'll raise the house value if you decide to sell. You going to work today?"

"No. I'd only be there for a couple of hours at this point. I'll have Danny do some lessons, then we'll try again tomorrow."

"Sounds good. I'm heading into the office. Should be back in time for supper. Want me to pick something up?"

She shook her head. "There isn't much here. I need to go to the grocery store."

"I'd rather you stayed inside."

"The store is within walking distance. We'll be fine."

Ryan didn't like her plans at all, but he wouldn't catch the perp by babysitting Maddy and his nephew. "Do you have pepper spray? A Taser?"

"I can add them to my shopping list."

"Stay around people. I'll install the cameras when I come home tonight." He searched her face for signs of worry. Not finding any, he headed to his car, wishing he could lock her up so she wouldn't become a victim.

All he wanted was to erase the horror of the last six months so Danny could be the carefree ten-year-old he should be. Ryan could do neither of these things.

At the office, he headed for the conference room where the feds had set up their base. "What's the plan?"

Lee glanced over from the case board. "If he continues in the same vein, another woman will disappear tonight. We need to enforce a curfew. No one out after dark unless going or coming from work. That seems to be when this guy moves."

"The folks in town won't like it," Bundt said. "They'll think you're infringing on their rights."

"Women are dying, Deputy." Starling narrowed her eyes. "Maybe fewer will die if they're locked safe in their homes."

"I'm not saying we shouldn't have a curfew; I'm simply stating how most of the townspeople will react. Sheriff?"

The sheriff stared at the photos of the victims on the case board. "I say we do an eight p.m. curfew. Let the people be upset. Their daughters and sisters are being hunted."

"Not to mention how close this perp has gotten to Miss Everton," Ryan added. "He'll succeed in taking her if we don't stop him. The curfew might at least slow him down." It also meant late nights for the sheriff's department. Someone would have to patrol to make sure the people were following the mandate.

The sheriff rose to his feet. "Good, I'll let the newspaper and TV stations know. I'll also drive around and make the announcement. Let's stop this guy already."

~

A curfew? He rolled his eyes as the sheriff drove up and down the streets shouting the news like Paul Revere. This definitely put a kink in his plans.

He drummed his fingers on his steering wheel. Maybe he'd lay low for a while. Fool the sheriff and the feds into thinking he'd moved on. Then, when they let down their guard, he'd take the biggest prize.

He hadn't anticipated leaving the body at the captain's place would have them moving into town. Getting to Maddy had just gotten a lot harder. The old woman who lived next door to her didn't miss much that went on in her neighborhood. Luring Maddy out when the time came would be the best way. It wouldn't be hard. Not with her being so nice and trusting.

He turned the key in the ignition and cruised the town, keeping an eye out for an easy take. Since he'd killed so many, most women now went around town with their hair covered. Several had simply gone to live somewhere else for a while. But, the people of this town weren't the brightest. Someone suitable would make a mistake, and he'd have another to fill his time until he got Maddy.

Chapter Nine

Maddy's eyes popped open. She lay without moving, straining her ears to hear what had awakened her. When no other sound came, her eyes drifted closed. The slam of the screened door in the back snapped them open again.

Someone had entered the house. Ryan? No, he'd said he had to work late. She glanced at the clock. A few minutes before midnight. It had to be someone who didn't know how difficult it was to keep the screen from banging.

Maddy stretched to grab the phone from her nightstand only to bring it back empty. She'd left it on the coffee table. Unless she could sneak in there undetected, she had no way of calling for help.

Danny. She threw off the blankets and tiptoed down the hall to his room. He slept like a baby. She eased his door closed so he would stay that way.

The scuff of a foot froze her in place as she held her breath. Her small house didn't have many places for her to hide. She slipped into the hall closet and pulled the door almost closed, leaving herself just enough room to peer out.

Footsteps went past her. Peering through the crack,

she spotted a man wearing a dark hoody step into her bedroom only to return seconds later. He stopped in front of the closet.

She clamped a hand over her mouth. Would he hear her breathing? She remained where she hid until he moved past.

Minutes later, the screen door banged again. The man cursed.

Maddy moved from the closet and dashed to the living room where she'd left her phone on the charger. Her fingers shook as she pressed 911.

"Operator. What is your emergency?"

"There's an intruder," she whispered, heading back to the closet. "He was inside, but now he's outside."

"Stay where you are. The police are on their way."

Her shoulders sagged. "Should I unlock the door for them? Oh, wait. The back door is unlocked."

"I'll let them know."

After what seemed like an eternity, the back door slammed, and someone called her name. "Maddy, it's me, Lance."

Thank God. She darted from her hiding place and into the kitchen. "Thank you for coming."

"An intruder?"

"Yes. He went down the hall and into my room. It's the second door on the right," she said, although he'd already started in that direction.

"Maddy, you should come see this."

Her steps lagged as she joined him in her room. On her pillow lay a red rose and a note that read, "I'm coming for you." Her legs gave way, and she crumbled to the floor.

Lance rushed to her side and tried to pull her into

his arms. She crawled away and struggled to her feet.

"I'm fine. Just shaken up." She allowed him to take her hand and lead her to sit on the bed. "He was in my room, Lance."

He took both her hands in his. "You're okay."

She nodded, realizing other than a moment of weakness, she really was okay. "Thank you for coming."

He laughed. "It's my job, and I wasn't far."

"Thank goodness. Would you like some coffee? Stay until I settle down or Ryan comes home?"

"Absolutely." He grinned and helped her up. "Actually, I'll make the coffee. You've had quite the night."

In the kitchen, Lance insisted she have a seat at the table. She watched as he opened and closed cupboards looking for the cups and coffee grounds.

"Everything you need is next to the refrigerator. It's like my small coffee bar." Actually, Alli had set everything there. Maddy didn't change a thing when she arrived. She didn't have the heart to. This was Alli's house. "There's creamer in the door of the fridge."

"Clever." Soon, he set a cup of coffee in front of each of them. He sat across from her, his gaze fixed on her face. "You're a brave woman."

"I hid." Smarter than brave.

"Which was smart." He echoed her thoughts.

She shrugged and took a small sip of her drink, relishing the heat as it passed over her tongue and into her throat. "Danny slept through it, thankfully. He's already seen so much, been through so much."

Lance nodded.

Maddy kept glancing at the door. Why hadn't Ryan come? He'd have heard about the intruder by now, right?

"The others are busy trying to catch this guy. I was the one on call which is why I'm here."

"There needs to be more law enforcement." She took another sip and eyed the door again. "Everyone is overworked."

"It's the way of things."

Maybe. She hated the exhaustion that Ryan wore like a worn-out sweatshirt.

A key turned in the lock of the front door. It banged open, and Ryan barged in. "Maddy!"

"I'm here." She jumped to her feet and ran into his open arms. "We're okay. Lance checked out the house. The killer left me a rose and a note." Her stomach churned.

"We haven't touched a thing," Lance said. "Where are the crime scene techs?"

"On their way. We had a shooting at the bar. That's why I'm late."

"There's coffee." Maddy stepped back.

"Danny?"

"Sleeping."

"Then I will have that coffee in just a minute."

~

When Ryan heard about the intruder, he'd wanted to rush to Maddy's side. Instead, he'd been stuck questioning witnesses at the local bar. Turned out to be a case of road rage between two bikers passing through town.

He marched into Maddy's room and stared at the killer's offerings. The perp had come close to nabbing her tonight. Why hadn't he?

"I hid in the closet," Maddy said when he asked. "Lance left. Said you weren't both needed here." She handed him a cup of coffee.

"Did Lance look around outside?"

"I don't know. Only inside, I think."

Ryan nodded, setting his cup on the table. "I'll be right back. Don't go outside." He clicked his flashlight from his belt and left through the back door, jumping as it slammed shut behind him. He really needed to fix that for her.

He shined the light around the ground. It had rained a bit, the ground now covered with a thin coating of sleet. There. Under Maddy's window, perfectly frozen was a footprint like the one he'd found at his place.

Lights signaled the crime techs' arrival. Ryan circled the house to the front, letting them know about the print. "I don't think he touched anything in the house other than the back doorknob. Pretty sure he's smart enough to have worn gloves."

Behind them arrived a black SUV. The two FBI agents stepped out. Stone-faced, they marched up the drive and into the house.

"Anything you can tell us at all, Miss Everton, will help," Starling said as Ryan entered.

"Dark pants, black hoodie. I didn't see his face."

"How tall?"

Maddy frowned. "About the captain's height, I think. Maybe a little shorter."

"Caucasian?"

"Yes." She'd caught a glimpse of his arm when he'd passed her hiding place. Just an inch above his glove and below his sleeve. "He came in, went to my room, then came back out and left. He cursed when the screen door slammed, but not enough that I'd recognize his voice."

"I'll fix that." Ryan picked his cup back up.

"Don't. The banging woke me up and alerted me that someone was inside. I don't ever want it fixed."

"Then we'll leave it." He smiled over the rim of his cup, glad to see she hadn't broken down over the night's events.

"Who responded to the 911 call?" Lee asked.

"Lance. He said he was on call tonight."

The two agents nodded.

Starling handed Maddy a card. "Call if you remember anything else?" Then, she spun and strode from the house, followed by her partner.

"They come and go quite quickly, don't they?" Maddy's frown deepened.

"Yes. They are very focused." He excused himself to check on Danny.

His nephew lay curled in a fetal position. His blankets had been kicked to the foot of the bed. Ryan pulled them up to the boy's chin and smoothed his hair from his face. Ten-years-old looked very young while sleeping. Thank God he hadn't woken up with the intruder in the house. Too much of this and he'd snap. How much could a child take?

He sat on the bed, overwhelmed by responsibility. When he'd received the call that his brother and his wife had been murdered, leaving Danny an orphan, he hadn't realized the work a child could be. Especially a traumatized one.

Add in a woman with a mission, hunted by a killer,

and the work tripled. What if he couldn't keep them safe?

"Are you okay?" Maddy whispered from the doorway.

"I'm not the one who almost faced a killer." He forced a smile.

"If he'd wanted to take me, it wouldn't have been very hard for him to find me."

True.

"Captain?" One of the crime scene techs joined them. "Got a second?"

"Yep." Ryan followed the man to the back door.

"Unless the scratches have always been here, the intruder picked the lock."

Ryan peered at the scratches around the lock. Time for an upgrade. "Maddy?"

"Those are new, I'm pretty sure." She paled. "I didn't hear him picking the lock."

"You wouldn't have. Not if you were sleeping." Ryan straightened. He'd wondered how the intruder had entered, thinking maybe Maddy had forgotten to lock the back door, so he was very glad she hadn't been that irresponsible. "I'll change the locks later today. The ones I have aren't easily picked."

Maddy sighed and returned to the table. She stared into her cup. "Empty, but it's too late for another."

"Go to bed. I can see these people out when they're finished."

She looked as if she wanted to argue but simply nodded and shuffled down the hall.

His cell vibrated. A text from the sheriff. Another woman taken, this one from her home. A house two doors down from Maddy's. Ryan's blood froze.

~

He was pretty sure Maddy had gotten his message. Especially, once she found out he'd nabbed her neighbor. The woman was a bit older than he preferred but fit the profile and would satisfy his hunger.

Taking the woman, after having broken into Maddy's home—these things would work in his favor. Maddy would spend her days terrified, and he'd swoop in like a knight and save her. He'd let her think that by loving him, the murders would stop. They wouldn't. His hunger was too big for that. But, he'd have her to come home to. She would help him present a normal life that wouldn't set off red flags to the community.

His latest acquisition stared up at him with wide eyes. She whimpered behind the gag.

It wasn't until he looked closer that he noticed the dark roots under the hair dye. He swore and paced the room. Just a fake, not even close to second prize.

His pace increased. She'd have to die. The question was…do it now or stick to his MO of three days?

Disgust ripped through him as the woman relieved herself on the blankets she lay on. Weak fool. The others hadn't done that until right after death.

He'd go to bed and rid the world of her when he woke up. With another glimpse of her, he stormed away. Let her lie in her mess. She'd freeze in the basement. Already a chill hung in the room. Maybe she'd be dead by morning and spare him the trouble.

In bed, the quilts pulled up to his chin against the cold night, he fell asleep trying to figure out how to get rid of the captain's kid. The boy had seen too much. Kids were observant. It wouldn't take much for the boy to recognize him if the kid saw him long enough.

Chapter Ten

Maddy scanned the playground on her way to the cafeteria. She shouldn't worry so about Danny. The school aides kept a close eye on the students, but with a killer on the loose, she couldn't help herself. After all, other than herself and the boy, no one had seen the man and lived.

The skin on the back of her neck prickled, and she increased her pace. Silly to be anxious in the middle of the day. The Abductor wouldn't enter a school during school hours. No one could enter the school without showing ID.

Seemed strange to see all brunette teachers in line to purchase their lunch, except for Maddy. She sighed and grabbed a tray. They were no closer to discovering the killer's identity then they were the day she arrived. She'd spoken to the new manager at the grocery store. It didn't seem plausible that the man behind the deaths would be in his fifties.

Her gaze flicked to the maintenance man. Maybe forty? She narrowed her eyes at his predatory stare. It could be him. He didn't seem to be paying a lot of attention to any of the other teachers.

He smirked and hurried out the double doors.

"That man gives me the creeps," a substitute teacher said. "I feel like he's undressing me with his eyes."

Maddy nodded, noting the woman's dark hair. Maybe she was wrong about Mr. Henderson being the killer. "Why hasn't anyone complained to the principal?"

"No law against staring."

Still creepy. Maddy held out her tray for fresh enchiladas made only for the staff by the wonderful lunch ladies. With food in hand, she headed to the teacher's lounge.

Mr. White glanced up from his lunch. "You doing okay?"

"Just fine." Maddy smiled and sat at the round table large enough for four. She wouldn't tell him about the intruder last night. He'd only make her take a few days off and, with winter break coming, she'd have enough time to sit around and do nothing but worry. It bothered her she hadn't been able to accomplish the goal she'd set for herself in coming to Misty Hollow. It was as if she'd failed Allison.

"How is Danny?"

"Getting through his grief little by little." She cut into her enchilada. "I think it helps that I'm staying with him for a while. It's a semblance of having parents, I guess."

"Not to mention your safety."

Maddy nodded, wishing he'd change the subject. It would be nice if work was a place she could escape the horror of being hunted. Instead, either she received pitying looks or questions. She could do without either.

As if he'd picked up on her thoughts, Mr. White

excused himself, mumbling something about a phone call.

The rest of her lunch time passed in silence as teachers came and went, but none starting up a conversation with her. Oh, she got the looks she hated, but at least no one started talking. She finished her lunch and went to collect her students from the playground.

"Danny sat alone during recess," one of the aides told her. "He said he feels fine, though."

"I am!" Danny crossed his arms. "Everyone needs to stop babying me."

"If you want to be treated older, then don't act like a pouting toddler." Maddy put a hand on his shoulder and smiled to take some of the sting from her words. "Miss Sally is only trying to help you."

"Sorry." He stepped to the end of the line.

Maddy shook her head, then led the class back to her room doing her best to understand that Danny was a hurting child and not a troublesome one. Some days were harder than others.

With one last sweep of the playground, she led her class inside. Since the day was early release, they didn't have long before school let out and teachers congregated in the media room for a meeting. Danny would spend the afternoon in the after-school program.

Her mind wandered during the meeting. No matter how much she tried to concentrate, she kept going back to the intruder the night before. The more she thought about him, the more she felt as if something about him seemed familiar. The way he walked, moved his head—something niggled at her. If only she could pinpoint what it was.

"Miss Everton?" Mr. White drew her attention back to her job. "Any thoughts?"

"Uh, regarding?"

"Holiday celebration. We're thinking of having each class sing a song, recite a poem, something of that nature." Worry creased his face. "Are you up to it?"

"Of course. We'll sing a song." The kids could learn one easily enough and be ready for the last day of school before break. It would be a welcomed distraction.

"Very good."

The meeting ended fifteen minutes early. Maddy rushed to her room to grab her backpack, then headed to the multi-purpose room to retrieve Danny. She stood in the doorway and scanned the small group of children.

"Is Danny in the bathroom?" She asked the woman who watched over the kids.

"Oh. Well, he went quite a while ago. I thought he'd returned." She tapped a boy on the shoulder. "Will you go check the boy's room and tell Danny that Miss Everton is ready to leave?"

The boy dashed away only to return without Danny. "Not there." He returned to his play.

"I'll have the front desk call him over the intercom." Maddy hurried to the school secretary. Minutes later with no Danny, she grew worried. Several of the teachers agreed to help look for him. When they'd scoured the entire school, it became apparent that Danny was not on the premises.

Maddy dug her phone out of her pack and called Ryan.

~

"Danny is missing."

Ryan's heart dropped. "What do you mean by missing?"

"He left the after-school program." Maddy's voice broke. "We've searched the entire school."

"I'm on my way." He hung up and sprinted to his car, shouting to the agents that he had a family emergency.

Had The Abductor changed his MO to children? Or just Danny because he'd seen too much?

He kept his eyes peeled for any sign of his nephew as he sped to the school. When he arrived out front, he saw Maddy and Mr. White standing outside by the flagpole.

"I'm so sorry." Tears spilled down Maddy's cheeks. "I sent him to the after-school program like he always does on early-release day. The lady watching over them said he went to the bathroom. She didn't know he hadn't returned until I arrived."

He'd have the woman fired for her negligence. "Show me."

With a nod and a sniff, she led him to the multi-purpose room where a young woman stood with a group of children clustered around her. Ryan gave her a death glare and continued to follow Maddy to the boy's restroom.

"Any sign of his backpack?" He asked, checking the five stalls.

"No. He must have it with him."

He shot her a look. "Why would he take it to the restroom?"

"I don't know." She lifted red-rimmed eyes to his. "Is it possible he ran away?"

"Maybe." Even while that thought filled him with

dread, it was better than his first thought of Danny being abducted. Where would he go?

His nephew didn't have any favorite places that Ryan knew of. He hardly had any friends, despite them living in Misty Hollow for a couple of months.

He huffed and marched for the door. "Come on."

"Where are we going?" Maddy raced to keep up with him.

"I'm not sure yet. We'll check the house first." He cut her a quick glance. "Do you have a gun?"

"Yes, but I don't carry it with me. I'm a teacher."

"When you aren't at school, you should have it with you. When you are working, keep it in your glove compartment."

Her eyes widened. "You think things are about to come to a head?"

"He took your neighbor. A woman older than the ones he usually takes. A woman who isn't a natural blonde. I believe he took her to frighten you." Ryan reached for the door handle as she rushed to the passenger side.

"Women are dying. I'm his target. Why hasn't he come for me?"

"I don't know." Ryan slid into the driver's seat as she climbed in on her side. "Be vigilant." He turned the key in the ignition, slapped his police light on top of his car, and sped away from the school.

"Danny!" Ryan barged into Maddy's house. Receiving no answer, he raced from room to room. He wasn't here.

Back in the living room, he clutched Maddy's shoulders and stared into her eyes. "You're with him every day. Has he mentioned a place? Somewhere he might be hiding?"

"He asks to stop for ice cream a lot. Would he go there?"

"Maybe. It is a public place, and I make sure he always has some money on him, just in case." Hope leaped within him. Danny would know to go somewhere public if he was frightened or followed. But why not stay at the school?

"We'll find him." Maddy reached over and took his hand. "This is a small town. He can't go far."

Unless someone took him away. Ryan forced a smile and gave her hand a squeeze. In his job, he saw all kinds of bad things happen to people, some of which were children. While he liked Maddy's optimism, her attempt to keep him from panicking, the odds of finding him were small.

Ryan found a parking spot two doors down from the ice cream shop. He headed for the shop with long strides, keeping a tight hold on Maddy's hand so she wouldn't fall behind.

A bell jingled as he shoved the door open. His gaze scanned the shop, settling on a child, back to the door, sitting at a table in the corner. "Danny?"

The boy whirled around. His eyes widened a split second before he launched himself at Ryan. "I knew you'd find me."

"Thanks to Miss Everton." He led him back to the table where a cardboard cup of chocolate ice cream sat half-eaten. "Why did you leave school?"

Maddy sat next to him, her gaze on Danny. "You scared us."

Tears welled in his eyes. "I saw him again."

"Who?" Ryan put a hand on Danny's.

"The man who attacked Miss Everton at the school. The same one who kept coming to our house. The man who wears a black hoodie." He trembled.

"Are you sure? Even I have a dark hoodie."

"I know who I saw." Danny crossed his arms.

"Okay. I believe you." Even if it wasn't the same man, it had frightened Danny enough to run. "You went to the bathroom with your backpack. Why?"

"I wanted to read in peace. When I saw it was almost time for the teacher meeting to end, I went out. That's when I saw him. He stood by the basketball hoops."

"Did he see you?"

"I don't think so, but I ran the other way and climbed the fence."

Ryan exhaled heavily and pulled his nephew into his arms. "You should have gone back inside."

"I was too scared to think right."

Ryan met Maddy's worried eyes over the boy's head. "How about we pick up a pizza on our way home?"

"That sounds like a great idea." Maddy rubbed Danny's back. "Pizza and a movie."

"I can stay up late?" Danny straightened, his face brightening.

Ryan laughed. "Just a little. You still have school tomorrow."

"Ugh."

"It's almost winter break. You'll survive." He ruffled Danny's hair. "No more running off. You find Miss Everton or another teacher if you get scared again. Promise?"

"Okay. I promise." He scarfed down the rest of his

ice cream and grabbed his backpack.

The idea that Danny might have actually seen The Abductor on the school grounds again plagued Ryan all the way home. The man grew bolder with each passing day.

Chapter Eleven

He glared at the fake blonde tied and gagged in front of him. What was he doing? He'd wasted valuable time with her when he could have been working with someone he actually wanted.

He eyed the gun in his hand, tempted to end it all as his fiancée, Sarah, had done a year ago. Her selfish act had turned his life upside down. Now, he searched for her replacement when he knew no such woman existed. Not even Maddy Everton could come close to his beloved Sarah. But, she might be the closest he'd find.

Even if he found another woman he wanted to spend his life with, it wouldn't quench his thirst for killing. Sarah had killed herself, saying his temper had made her do it. Her letter said he'd killed her. It didn't take long for him to kill after that. He had a knack.

He'd waited and waited for Maddy to come out of the school. When too many others exited the building, he'd had to leave. Somehow, he'd get her alone.

"Might as well get this over with." He raised the gun. Since he didn't really care about making this killing personal, he pulled the trigger, shooting the woman between the eyes. Quick and merciful.

He knew just the place to put her.

~

"Stand back." Ryan held his arm in front of Maddy and Danny.

"What is it? Who is that?"

"Take Danny back inside."

"But—"

"Maddy, please." The request came out more as a growl this time. "I'll explain in a minute." He reached for the phone clipped to his belt as he stepped closer to the car.

How had someone put the woman inside? Ryan recognized the woman as Maddy's neighbor. The bullet hole between her eyes left no doubt she was dead. He always locked his car. Had he been so consumed with worry over Danny that he forgot?

He dialed the sheriff. "I've got the latest missing woman in the back of my car."

"She alive?"

"No, sir."

"Are you saying the killer put her there?"

"I am."

"I'm sending someone your way. I'm in the middle of something. If I can get away, I'll join you. Where is Miss Everton?"

"In the ice cream shop with my nephew. He saw the man at the school and took off in a panic."

"Catch this guy." The sheriff hung up.

While he waited for whoever was free to come, he motioned for Maddy to step outside and filled her in. "I don't know how long I'll be. Can you call someone to give you a ride home?"

"It isn't far. We can walk. We'll make it before

dark."

"Did you grab your gun when we were at the house?" When she nodded, he continued, "Keep your gun where you can grab it quickly."

"I'll walk with one hand on it. Be careful, Ryan." She stepped back inside to collect Danny.

He watched them stroll hand in hand down the sidewalk until they turned a corner out of sight. By then, the FBI and Deputy Miller had arrived.

"Who has access to your vehicle?" Starling asked.

"No one." Ryan knew he'd locked the car.

"No alarm?"

"It's an older model. The alarm has long since broken." He didn't think he needed it fixed in a town like Misty Hollow. How wrong he was.

"Why your car?" Agent Lee asked, peering at the body through the window before opening the door.

"Guess someone has a grudge against me." Ryan rubbed his hands down his face.

"Ain't this something?" Deputy Miller folded his arms across his slight paunch. "Until last year, when the sheriff's wife's brother went nutso from a brain tumor, nothing much happened in this town. Now, we have our very own serial killer."

"You sound as if that excites you." Ryan narrowed his eyes.

"Not excite exactly, but it does liven things up." He grinned and shrugged. "Boring most of the time. I heard through the grapevine you followed the killer here from Langley."

"I did."

"Might want to talk to Bundt. He lives in Oak Ridge. He might know something."

Ryan had lived in that town, too, and didn't know much. Why would Bundt? Still, it wouldn't hurt to talk to him. Maybe something had surfaced that hadn't made it to the Misty Hollow sheriff's department yet. Slim chance. The department here lived and breathed this case.

"What's happened?" Bundt rushed toward them.

Speaking of the devil. "Body dumped in my car."

The deputy's brows rose. "This guy has something against you."

"Maybe I'm getting close."

"Maybe. Sorry I'm late. Had a flat after driving up the mountain."

"For what?" Ryan didn't remember any calls coming in.

"Just routine. I make the drive once or twice a week, same as through town."

"Instead of driving around, how about helping find this guy?"

"I'm doing that, too." Bundt smirked. "You're the captain. If you want me pounding the pavement, I will. But, has it occurred to you the man we're looking for might be hiding out on that mountain? While you're babysitting the pretty teacher and Miller is searching the internet, I'm actually out looking."

Heat rose up Ryan's neck. "Are you accusing me of not doing my job?"

"No more so than you are me."

"If you two roosters are done showing your feathers, can we finish things up here?" Starling frowned.

Sounded good to him. The deputy always seemed to get on Ryan's bad side. His phone buzzed. A text from the sheriff implementing a mandatory curfew from dark to dark. If you aren't headed to or from a job, you are not to be on the streets.

Ryan turned to find a reporter's microphone shoved in his face.

~

"I don't like him," Danny said of Deputy Bundt as he passed them on the sidewalk.

"Well, that's unfortunate. Since your uncle works with him, you'll be seeing him around." She didn't much care for the deputy either. Even passing on the sidewalk, he seemed to step into her personal bubble. A space very few were allowed into.

She turned as Lance moved to cross the street. His gaze locked on her. Gone was the friendliness he usually bestowed on her. His features hardened. A chill that had nothing to do with the winter air went through her.

"Can we still get a pizza?" Danny asked.

"We'll pass right by there." Her stomach rumbled, and Ryan would be hungry when he finally got home.

Her phone buzzed. Ryan asked whether they'd made it home. She replied that they were stopping to pick up a pizza. His answer was that the sheriff had set a curfew.

She glanced at the sky. They'd have to hurry.

By the time they reached her house, pizza in hand, the sun kissed the top of the mountain. "Just in time, buddy." She locked the door behind them and set the pizza on the table before making sure all the cameras were working properly. Satisfied they were, she grabbed a couple of paper plates. "Go pick a movie."

"Yay." Danny thundered off, returning with a

movie about dinosaurs.

As soon as he turned on the TV, Ryan's face filled the screen. "Yes, this is the latest missing woman. Other than that, I have nothing I can tell you other than a curfew has been set."

The reporter kept badgering him until Ryan turned and marched away. When she tried to approach Lance or Deputy Miller, they each put up a hand and shook their head.

"Is my uncle a movie star now?" Danny paused in switching over to the movie.

"No." Maddy chuckled. "He's doing his job as Captain."

"Why did we walk home?"

She couldn't very well tell him the complete truth. Not after the scare he'd received earlier that day. "He was called in to work a while longer."

Danny seemed to accept her answer and turned on the movie. Once he settled on the sofa, Maddy peered out the front window, then pulled the blinds tight. She wouldn't rest well until The Abductor was caught and behind bars.

She jumped at every noise that didn't come from the television. Jerked upright every time headlights shone past the window. Ridiculous. The killer wouldn't drive up, and she knew from experience that the creak of the back door always let her know when someone entered.

Relief washed over her when Ryan's key rattled in the lock. "The pizza is still warm."

"That sounds wonderful. Let me lock these up, and I'll be right back." Gun and badge in hand, he headed for the room he shared with Danny.

While he was gone, Maddy set two slices of pizza on a plate and grabbed him a beer from the fridge. He'd earned one for sure.

"A woman after my own heart." He gave a tired smile at the sight of the beer.

"How did the woman get in your car?" She asked after making sure Danny was engrossed in his movie.

"I don't know. No one other than me has keys to my vehicle. It would have to be someone very skilled to break in."

"Can you?"

"Sure. I have tools." His eyes widened. "We need to consider that our killer is a tradesman. Someone who knows how to get in and out of places unseen, pick locks, that sort of thing. And reckless. He put the body in my car during daylight."

Maddy thought back to the form she'd seen passing the closet where she hid. "A big man, about your size. At least from the back. I couldn't see his hair color, only that he's Caucasian." She gasped. "He has blue eyes. I remember seeing them through the slits in the mask."

"That's a start." Ryan grinned. "Half the male population of Misty Hollow most likely has blue eyes, but it's definitely more than we had."

"What if he doesn't live in Misty Hollow? What if he only hunts here?"

"Or works here." Ryan fell heavily into a kitchen chair. "It's still like looking for a needle in a haystack."

She sat across from him. "The FBI don't have any clues?"

"If they do, they aren't sharing." He wrapped his hands around his empty beer bottle.

"I thought they were working with you, not against you."

"They've taken over, which really irks Sheriff Westbrook. It's as if they don't think this small law enforcement department can actually catch this guy."

Worry and exhaustion creased his handsome face. The ending theme song to the movie Danny watched started to play. Maddy put her hand over Ryan's. "Take Danny to bed. You need the sleep. I'll clean up here and head to my room in a few minutes."

"I don't like leaving you alone."

"The doors are locked, the windows secure. You're right down the hall. I'll be fine." She smiled. "Last time he broke in, you weren't here. This man wouldn't dare try coming in with you here."

He tilted his head, his eyes warming. "You're something else, Madison Everton. You come to Misty Hollow to find out who killed your sister, dive into caring for a hurting little boy, and while you've faltered a time or two, you keep going."

Her face flushed. "I've been more scared than I can ever remember. And yes, I have a heart for kids or I wouldn't be a teacher. But, I've done nothing to gather any information on who killed Allison. Instead, I'm living with the captain just to stay safe. I can't say it feels like I'm something else."

He chuckled and took his hands off the bottle and wrapped them around hers. "Then you'll have to trust me." He lifted her hand to his lips and placed a gentle kiss in her palm. "Get some sleep, Maddy. We have work to do."

"You have an idea?"

"It's most likely foolish, definitely a risk, but yes, I

have a plan. You in?"

"Absolutely." Time to bring a killer to his knees.

Chapter Twelve

Ryan had breakfast ready by the time Maddy shuffled into the kitchen. "Sleep well?"

"Not really. My mind wouldn't shut off." She slumped into a chair. A split second later, he set a cup of coffee in front of her.

"I've called you out of school for the day."

"What?" Maddy scowled. "Don't you think that's something you should have discussed with me?" She glared first at him, then at her innocent cup of coffee.

"Relax, grumpy morning person. I told you last night I was coming up with a plan, and I did." He set a plate of scrambled eggs and bacon on the table. "You awake enough to hear it? I'd like to tell you before Danny joins us."

"Sorry. Yes, tell me." She breathed deep of the coffee, then took a sip. He still should've discussed her missing work before calling in to the school. Everything was supposed to be done on the computer. But, considering the circumstances, if he'd called Mr. White, the principal would have easily given her the day off.

"I'm sending Danny to stay with my parents until this case is resolved. I called them last night and they agreed to help. He'll be safer, and we'll be able to focus without worrying about him." He sat across from her with his own plate.

"But Christmas…"

"I really hope to have this completed by then. I've ordered his Christmas presents online, so however things go, he'll have those in time."

"Then what?"

He blinked a few times as if trying to decipher her question. "What's next for us? We start talking loudly in public places about this guy. When we return from my parents' place, we'll have lunch at the diner. Word spreads fast in this town. Someone will let the perp know we're gunning for him."

"We don't know enough to be a threat."

"He doesn't know that. There aren't many blondes left in Misty Hollow. Most have left town for the time being. He might move on. Then, we could lose him for good."

She nodded. Her coworker had taken a leave of absence, but Maddy wasn't sure where she'd gone. "You're right. It's risky, but I'm tired of waiting in limbo." His plan could get one or both of them killed.

"Great. I'll get Danny up and fed, then we'll hit the road. It'll take two hours, round trip, and I'm sure my parents will want to visit a bit." He pushed to his feet and set his dishes in the sink before heading to his room.

Maddy sighed and shoved aside her half-empty plate. It seemed hard to believe that The Abductor would happen to hear, or care, that they were closer to him than he thought. Since they had nothing other than his gender and eye color, faking such knowledge wouldn't be easy. They weren't dealing with a dumb man.

She rinsed the dishes and set them in the dishwasher before heading to her room. Hopefully, she had time for a quick shower. It would take more than coffee to get her going this morning. Ryan must have had the same idea because she heard the shower come on in the guest bathroom seconds before she turned on hers.

The patter of bare feet signaled Danny's race to the kitchen where he'd no doubt take his breakfast to the living room in front of the television. She could take her time getting ready.

Maddy turned the shower as hot as she could get it, dropped her pajamas on the floor, and then stepped under the spray, lifting her face. She imagined her fears and worries washing down the drain with the soap and shampoo. She imagined her sister doing the same thing. If Alli hadn't wanted her independence so desperately, she'd be alive in this shower, most likely dreaming of her future. Instead, it was her older sister here set on revenge, justice.

Her heart felt as if clutched in a fist, squeezed and pounded. Alli had been her best friend. Maddy had loved having a sister just two years younger. Now, someone had taken that all away from her.

Cutting off the water with a strong twist of the handle, she reached blindly for the towel on the rack. She scrubbed her face and body as if she could rid herself of all that was evil.

A knock on the door signaled she needed to speed things up. With the towel wrapped around her, she headed for the walk-in closet. Maddy had brought few of her own clothes since she and Alli wore the same size. She chose a pair of skinny jeans and a baggy sweater that fell below her rear end. Her long hair was swept back into a ponytail. Since she wasn't heading to work, she skipped putting on makeup. Then, dropping the gun into her backpack, she rushed from the room and joined Ryan and Danny in the front room.

~

Oh, the look on the captain's face when he'd discovered the woman's body sitting upright in the backseat of his car was priceless. He'd hoped Maddy would also catch a glimpse but no such luck. The captain had shuffled her and the boy away quickly.

He drummed his fingers on his desk. The latest time frame hadn't been three days. But, she could never be a replacement for Sarah, so it didn't really matter. He did need someone new, though. Maybe someone from another town? Shake things up a bit?

The women of Misty Hollow, at least the ones he hadn't killed, were as skittish as newborn colts. Toss in the mandatory curfew, and the pickings were slim indeed.

At least he didn't live in Misty Hollow. The curfew wouldn't affect him if he chose to take a woman from a nearby city.

He groaned, stood, and stretched. As much as he didn't want to, he had to leave for work. Making his boss suspicious was the last thing he wanted to do. Things needed to stay routine as much as possible.

Snatching his car keys from the table by the front door, he headed for his car, whistling a tune he'd heard on the radio recently. The melancholy of the day before had fled in light of the torment he saw on the captain's face. The man was going to crack under the pressure. Same as the other yahoos in Misty Hollow's law enforcement.

He'd keep them running in circles until the time came for him to snatch Maddy. Then, he'd leave and find another town to terrorize.

~

"I don't want to stay with Grandma and Grandpa," Danny whined from the back seat. "I want to spend Christmas with you."

Ryan glanced in the rearview mirror. "I'm doing all I can to make sure that happens. You'll be safer there. No bad guy. This will give me more time to catch him. Don't you want him caught?"

"Yeah." Danny sighed as if the weight of the world rested on his thin shoulders. "What about school?"

"I'll make sure you have your lessons." Maddy smiled over her shoulder.

Danny frowned and stared out the window. "Why are we driving my teacher's car?"

"Because mine is being cleaned." No way would he let Danny ride on the same seat where a woman's body had been staged. Since she hadn't been killed in the car, there'd been very little blood to clean up, but his car was a crime scene. At least for the moment.

"Don't you like my car?" Maddy asked.

"It's okay."

"Too many changes," Ryan muttered.

She nodded. "Things will settle down eventually."

"You'd better come back for me," Danny said. "Don't leave me like my parents did."

"They didn't leave you on purpose. They were taken from you." His hands tightened on the steering wheel. The man who'd killed them during a break-in now sat behind bars for twenty years. Not nearly long enough, in his opinion. Locking him up wouldn't bring back Ryan's brother and sister-in-law. Same as stopping The Abductor wouldn't bring back the women he'd murdered, but it was something.

By the time he pulled into his parents' driveway, both Maddy and Danny had dozed off. His mother stepped onto the porch, her hands shoved into the pockets of the dress she wore. Concern creased her forehead.

Ryan exited the car, leaving the other two sleeping. "Thank you, Mom."

"We're happy to see that dear boy again. Who's with you?" She peered around him.

"His teacher. Her sister was killed, and now the killer is after her. She's been staying with me and Danny so I can protect her." Hopefully. Some days he doubted very much that he could.

"Bring them in. You've time for lunch, right? I've a ham and cheese casserole ready to come out of the oven."

He thought for a minute, then decided they could hit the diner for supper. Might be more people then to hear their false information. "Be right back." He jogged to the car and woke up Maddy and Danny.

"Lunch?" She frowned. "I thought we were—"

"We'll go for supper. Mom has already fixed something."

"Okay. I'm taking your lead on this."

He laughed. "That's good since I'm the law enforcement here."

A tinge of pink glowed on her cheeks. "Sorry. I'm

used to being the boss in the classroom."

He glanced up to see a glimmer of interest in his mother's eyes. She'd be trying to matchmake for sure. Let her. As much as he'd become used to seeing Maddy's face each morning and night, she'd be headed back home once the perp was caught.

"Welcome. It's always nice to meet a friend of my son's." Mom beamed at Maddy. "Especially such a pretty one."

"Teachers aren't pretty." Danny hugged his grandmother, then marched into the house.

Maddy's brows rose before she burst into laughter. "Well, then, I guess I've been put in my place."

"I think you're pretty," Ryan whispered from behind her. He smiled as she gasped. "Let's go visit a bit until lunch." He took her hand and led her past his grinning mother into the living room where his father snored from his recliner. "Dad?"

"Hey." His eyes popped open. "You didn't waste any time getting here. Who's this?"

Ryan repeated the answer he'd given his mother.

"Catch this guy." Dad returned his chair to an upright position. "He needs to be stopped, son. Back in my day, we had a serial killer similar to this guy. Had to set up a sting operation with an undercover female cop to catch him."

"I'm the bait." Maddy lowered herself onto the sofa.

Dad shook his head. "What are you thinking, son? It's too dangerous to use a civilian."

"We can't use anyone else. This guy is already fixated on Maddy." He hated deliberately putting her in danger, but she'd done that herself when she'd come to

Misty Hollow. "I won't let her out of my sight."

"Make sure you don't."

"I'm armed," Maddy said. "I'll be fine."

"Who knows what he does to the women during those three days." Dad glanced from Ryan to Maddy. "Terrible things."

"They don't seem to have been sexually assaulted, beaten, or starved, Dad. He takes care of them until he's finished with whatever he wanted them for."

"Why?"

He shrugged. "I guess we'll find out when we catch him."

"Don't worry about Danny. We'll take good care of him. I still have my gun."

"I don't think anyone is coming for him. It's Maddy he wants."

"Have her stay, too."

Maddy frowned. "Thank you for the offer, sir, but I didn't come here to hide. I came to seek justice for my sister."

"Can't get justice if you're dead."

She glanced at Ryan, a request for help in her eyes.

"We've no other options, Dad." Ryan kept his gaze on Maddy, his worry magnified tenfold in his heart.

Chapter Thirteen

Ryan led Maddy to the only available booth in Lucy's Diner. A small, two-person one in the back. He sat where he could see the door.

She wasn't law enforcement, but Maddy didn't like her back to the door any more than Ryan did. Her skin prickled. The only saving grace was the fact The Abductor didn't usually shoot the women, so she wouldn't get a bullet in the back.

The chatter of the full diner would make it hard for anyone to hear Ryan's plan. "I don't think this is going to work."

"It will. First, we mention something of importance to our server, who will then pass it on to a coworker and so on. It's how small towns work." He grinned and reached for two laminated menus in a holder on the table and handed one to Maddy. "Here comes our server."

A young woman with Katelyn printed on her name tag set two glasses of ice water on the table.

"We're getting very close to catching this guy. I wouldn't worry too much—" Ryan smiled at the server.

"You know who he is?" Katelyn's eyes widened. "Because once he's caught, my friends will come back."

"I can't divulge that information." He kept his smile in place.

How did he do that? "Since he seems to have me on his radar, I'm ecstatic you're getting close. Is he local?" Maddy arched a brow.

"I can't say."

She raised her voice. "Since I'm the one being stalked, I think I deserve to know who you suspect."

The noise in the diner lowered as patrons glanced sideways toward the booth where Maddy and Ryan sat.

"Are y'all ready to order?" Katelyn's pencil poised over her pad. "We're busy tonight."

"I'll have the chicken fried steak with extra gravy." Maddy closed her menu.

"I'll have the same." Ryan put both menus back in the holder.

Katelyn rushed away.

Maddy didn't know what else to say, still waiting to take her cue from Ryan.

"I didn't want to say too much in front of the waitress." He leaned against the back of the booth, his arms crossed. "With all the women who have disappeared, the perp has left enough clues that, yes, we believe we know who he is."

"Tell me." She said loudly, then lowered her voice and leaned over the table.

He shook his head, glancing at the other diners who had completely stopped talking by this time. "Later. Not here. Too many ears. There's bound to be someone who can read lips."

She lifted her water glass to hide her smile. Acting was kind of fun. Unfortunately, the circumstances for the game they played was anything but enjoyable. Her smile faded. What if their plan didn't work? Ryan could be jeopardizing his job. Word was bound to get back to the sheriff about their conversation.

"Excuse me." She slid from the booth and hurried to the ladies room. Inside, she stepped into a stall, locked the door, and sat, needing a moment of peace. She balanced her elbows on her knees and her chin in her hands. Yes, she definitely had second thoughts about what they were doing.

"That's what they said." A woman's voice, Katelyn's, she thought, spoke upon entering the room.

"If the authorities know who this guy is, why aren't they arresting him? Saying something on the news?" Another woman said. "We have a right to know."

Maddy froze, holding her breath to avoid discovery. If they saw her without Ryan, they'd bombard here with questions she couldn't answer.

"Well, the sheriff is out there having supper with one of the deputies. I'm going to demand to know what's going on."

"No, Lucy. I don't think the captain wanted the news to get out."

"Then he shouldn't have been speaking about it in public."

The two women left, leaving the room clear for her to emerge from the stall. The sheriff was in the diner? Maddy hadn't seen him or a deputy when she'd entered. She also hadn't been paying a lot of attention to folks at the tables or in the other booths.

She opened the door and peered out. Katelyn and the diner owner, Lucy, were nowhere in sight. Maddy rushed back to the booth.

"The sheriff is here with a deputy. Lucy is going to demand that he tells who The Abductor is."

Ryan frowned. "This isn't good. I'm so desperate to catch this guy I didn't think things through."

"It wasn't a bad plan. We didn't factor in the reactions of those who would hear us." She sat up straight as Katelyn delivered their meals.

"Please don't repeat what I said." Ryan glanced up. "And tell others to remain quiet. We don't want to tip the guy off. If he finds out, he'll disappear."

Maddy didn't think Katelyn would abide by his request, but it was worth a shot. Her phone buzzed. She fished it from her purse. A text from an unknown number.

There is no chance that my identity is known. What kind of game are you and the captain playing? You don't want to make me angry.

She gasped and turned the phone so Ryan could see the screen. "He's here," she whispered.

~

Ryan leaped from the booth. His sharp gaze roamed through the building. He knew all these people, by face if not by name. Which one was the killer?

"Captain." The sheriff waved from a few booths over where he sat with Bundt. "A word, please."

Squaring his shoulders, Ryan marched to the booth and slid in next to Bundt, who gave him a smug look. "Sir, I believe the—"

"I'll do the talking." Sheriff Westbrook's features appeared set in stone. "I think you're too close to this case."

"How so?"

"You followed our perp here. Now, you're talking about the investigation where dozens of people can hear."

"That was the idea." Ryan hitched his chin. "It's time to draw the perp into the open. Put pressure on him. The more people out there looking, the better."

"It won't work," Bundt said. "These are country and mountain people, not the police."

"These people have spines of steel. They'll fight to protect their own. If I did know the identity of The Abductor and let them know, they'd string him up before we arrested him. We have to flush him out so the killings stop." Nothing they said would change his mind. "Do you want to see Madison Everton's body dumped like her sister and the others?"

"You know I don't." The sheriff folded his arms on the table.

"Listen to me. Maddy received a text. The killer is here. He heard our conversation."

The sheriff stood and barked orders. "No one leaves this building. Deputy, lock the doors. Hostess, anyone left in the last fifteen minutes?"

"Just the Olsons," she said.

Too old to be the one they looked for. Ryan slid from the booth to let Bundt out. The deputy hit him with his shoulder as he passed. How long would the man be upset that Ryan got the captain position?

"Captain, start asking questions of every male who fits the description previously given by Miss Everton."

"Yes, sir." Pleased they were finally doing something constructive without waiting for the feds to tell what the next step was, Ryan made note of every fit male between the ages of twenty-five and forty.

Starling and Lee wouldn't be pleased the sheriff didn't call them right away, but that was the sheriff's problem. Ryan didn't care about protocol as long as the killer was caught and stopped.

"What about Miss Everton?" Bundt glanced her way as he headed for the back door.

"She stays. I want to see the text." The sheriff headed her way.

Ryan spent the next few minutes pulling aside every man in the place that fit the body type of the intruder Maddy had seen. Then, he eliminated those without blue eyes.

"Why are we being detained?" One man crossed his arms, his expression defiant. "You can't possibly think one of us is a killer." He glanced down the line of five men. "We live here."

"Just a few questions. Please be patient. I'll try and make this as quick as possible. Empty your pockets and place everything on the table. Unlock your cell phones." Somebody in the place had texted Maddy. Find out who, and they had their man.

The sheriff sat in the booth Ryan had vacated, an intense look on his face as he questioned Maddy. Bundt mingled with the other guests, answering questions without really saying anything.

Once all of the men had emptied their pockets, Ryan scrolled through their most recent text messages. The warning to Maddy hadn't come from one of the phones in front of him. "None of you have another phone?" Short of frisking them, which he had no grounds to do, he had to rely on their word.

All five shook their heads. After grilling each one individually, Ryan still had nothing.

"No one knows anything." Bundt stepped next to him. "No one saw anything. They heard nothing of interest except for your ridiculous conversation with Maddy."

"He's here. I know it." Ryan scanned the room again, all eyes in the place on him and the deputy. "Where's Miller?"

"Holding down the office while we waste time here."

"Do you have a better idea?" Ryan scowled. "I don't see you coming up with any ideas."

"The feds are here." He jerked his chin toward the door. "Guess I'll go let them in so they can do exactly what we just finished doing." He marched away.

The sheriff exited the booth where Maddy sat and went to greet the feds. Ryan mentally wished him luck. If the fierce expression on Starling's face was any indication, the man would receive a lecture for sure.

"Nothing?" Maddy joined Ryan.

"Not yet."

"He's here. He has to be or he wouldn't have heard our conversation." Her mouth dropped open. "You don't think we have a recorder on us or something, do you?"

He shook his head, chuckling. "This isn't a James Bond movie. Besides, if you'd have come that close to the killer, you wouldn't be standing here with me."

~

What a bunch of idiots. He'd been standing right there with them. It took all his self-control not to burst into laughter. Instead, he stood there and waited for one of them to tell him what to do while the woman he really wanted stood mere feet away.

With the captain rarely leaving her side, snatching her would be quite the challenge. Still, his intelligence would win in the end.

His gaze fell on the teenage daughter of one of the townspeople. Blonde but too young. He needed someone more mature than a mere child. A woman in her twenties came from the kitchen. He smiled. The hostess would be perfect for now.

She blushed and ducked her head when she caught him staring. Then, she glanced up through lowered lashes. The little flirt.

Smiling, he tossed her a wink. Later, sweetheart. He'd kept himself pure since Sarah, waiting for the perfect woman...Maddy. But this pretty little thing was a temptation for sure. No, stay focused on the prize. She'll be worth it.

He turned and caught Maddy's anxious gaze. She was studying every man in the place as if she could pick him out of the crowd. No chance. If she could, she would have told the captain who he was already.

He smiled, receiving a shaky one in return. She reminded him so much of Sarah it felt like a stab of a heated iron bar to the heart. Red, hot, and throbbing like the love they'd shared. For the first time in a long time, he felt as if he might have found something special again. The time would be soon. All he needed was the opportunity.

Chapter Fourteen

Ryan stared in astonishment at the sheriff. "What do you mean you're putting me on leave?"

"Exactly what I said. You've gotten too close to this case by moving Miss Everton into your home—I mean, her home now. Anyway—" he waved a dismissive hand, "the feds say you're becoming a hindrance. Look on the positive side...you can provide twenty-four-hour protection to Miss Everton. You'll still receive your pay."

Small consolation, but the sheriff was right. Ryan could keep an eye on Maddy at all times this way. "Okay." He started to stand.

"Hold on. I don't want you completely locked out of this case. The hostess from the diner disappeared last night."

"So, the killer *was* there."

"Maybe." Sheriff Westbrook folded his hands on top of the desk. "I'm going with the idea that, yes, he was there. It galls me that he's playing us."

"Sir? This man is always one step ahead of us. What if he's on the case?"

"What are you insinuating?" He frowned.

"Nothing at this moment." He motioned toward the

glass window dividing the sheriff's office from the bullpen. "Bundt and Miller both fit the shape of the man Maddy saw in her house."

"It's risky accusing one of the deputies, but I also have the feeling the killer is a lot closer than we ever thought."

"What do you know about them?"

"Both live in Langley, wanted to work in a small town, openings became available, and here they are." He sat back in his chair and crossed his arms. "Both were here before you, who also fits the profile."

"Except for the fact I was there when Maddy was attacked."

"Except for that."

"I plan on doing some deep digging into their backgrounds—" Ryan glanced up again at the feds who entered the building. "Without their knowledge."

The sheriff nodded. "I'll go along with that for now, but we'll have to tell them if you find anything of importance. Your main priority is Miss Everton. Now, I need to catch up with what those two yahoos have found out...if anything."

Dismissed, Ryan grabbed a few things he would need from his desk, laptop mainly. With a curt nod, he strode past the feds out to his car. Inside, he sat and drummed his hands on the steering wheel. The sheriff had actually given him the right to dig into the past lives of the two deputies.

Since the perp seemed to have Ryan in his sights, Ryan's mind settled on Bundt. The man clearly didn't like him since he'd been overlooked for the job of captain, if he'd ever had a chance. No matter that Ryan was better qualified for the job, the deputy made it clear how he felt. Maybe Miller felt the same way.

He turned the key in the ignition. Maddy was good with a computer. Together, they might actually discover something to move the case along. With another woman missing, they were running on a short amount of time.

~

"You really think Lance or Miller might be the killer?" Maddy's brows drew together. "I went on a date with Lance. He could have taken me then, and Miller might be a bit bigger than the man I saw."

"Hoodies cover up a lot, especially baggie ones." He set his laptop on the table. "Want to help me dig?"

"Sure." She retrieved her own laptop from her room and set it at the table across from him. "I'm sorry you were relieved from duty."

"Only officially." He grinned. "Unofficially, I'm still working on catching this guy."

If they caught him. The thought of living in fear, waiting to be pounced on, niggled at her like a cancer. She didn't want to live that way. "I'd focus on Lance. Miller wasn't at the diner last night to hear our conversation and send me that text." She shuddered thinking she'd gone out with the man who might possibly want her dead.

That was also what kept her from believing it could be Lance. If Bundt was the killer, then why hadn't he abducted her then? Too many questions. She groaned and covered her head with her hands.

"We will get him," Ryan said softly.

"Too many women have already died."

"We have to keep him from killing more."

She lifted her eyes to meet his. "It's taking too

long."

"Yes, it is, which is why I'm convinced it has to be someone on the case." He pressed his lips together.

True, but that didn't ease the prickles up and down her spine. She opened the laptop and started searching for anything she could find on Lance Bundt. "You've been here six months and don't know him?"

Ryan glanced up from his keyboard. "We aren't exactly friends. If it's not related to this case, we don't talk."

"Hmm." She didn't talk to all her coworkers either. "Lance was married until earlier this year. His wife died by suicide. She used his gun."

That caught Ryan's attention. "That might explain why he chose to work in Misty Hollow. The other officers would have looked at him differently."

Maddy's heart lodged in her throat when the photo of his wife appeared on her screen. Long blond hair, hazel eyes, wide smile.

"His deceased wife could be my sister." She turned her laptop for him to see.

"Holy cow." His wide-eyed gaze met hers. "He's trying to replace his dead wife."

"If—and without proof it's a big if—Lance is our guy." She turned the laptop back around and stared at her doppelgänger. A woman who looked a lot like Allison, too. Ryan's theory made a lot of sense. "Why is he waiting to take me? Why keep taking other women if it's me he wants?"

"He enjoys the thrill of abducting and killing." A muscle ticked in his jaw. "Even if he takes you, even if he somehow wants to keep you, he won't stop killing. He'll move on to greener pastures, taking you with him." Concern flickered in his eyes. "If he does get to you, do whatever he wants, say whatever he wants to hear. Stay alive until I can find you."

Was it possible that Ryan cared for her more than his job required? Her vision blurred. His words sounded straight out of a romance novel. "I don't intend on dying anytime soon." Of course, neither had Alli.

"Good." His eyes twinkled. "Danny would be very sad that his favorite teacher died."

And there it was. A single sentence to erase the one from before, reinforcing the fact that she was just a potential victim and he her bodyguard.

Just as well. Now was not the time for romance, especially since she probably wouldn't stay in Misty Hollow past the current schoolyear. She returned to her online search, squelching down the tiny niggle of hope that Ryan cared for her more than as his nephew's teacher.

Did she care for him? Yes. More than she should, both him and Danny. If Ryan's feelings didn't match her growing ones for him, it would make it easier to leave Misty Hollow. Why then did that idea put a hitch in her breath?

Further searching didn't reveal any more surprises. Maddy stood and stretched, her neck sore from bending over the keyboard. "Now what? Do you confront Lance?"

"No, but I am sending the sheriff an email with what we've found. Let him and the feds take it from there." He clasped his hands and stretched his arms above his head. "Want to take a drive past his house? He shouldn't be there. Since I'm on leave, he'll have had to take up the slack."

"Let's go." She grabbed her backpack and followed him outside. "How do you know where he lives?"

"I saw it in his files. As his supervisor, I had access." He opened the passenger door for her, then jogged to the driver's side.

Maddy prayed they weren't wasting their time by focusing on Lance while someone else continued to kill. "The killer has to have a place to stash these women for the three days."

"First thing I plan on looking for when we get there. A cellar would work, and a lot of the houses around here have them, or a basement they use for a storm shelter." He flashed her a grin. "We're on the right track. I feel it." Ryan reached over and squeezed her hand.

She wished she shared his enthusiasm. If Lance was The Abductor, it explained a whole lot of things. But, was it too easy?

While Ryan drove to the address on his GPS, Maddy stared out the window as they left the mountain and trees with skeletal fingers and drove past fields of dirt, waiting for spring planting. She shivered and pulled her coat closer around her shoulders. The gray day set the perfect backdrop for snooping around someone's property. *Alli, we're going to get him. I promise.*

Ryan pulled up in front of small, brick house on a nice-sized lot. The house had been built into a hill, the perfect place to have a basement. No cars sat in the driveway. No dog barked at them from the fence-enclosed backyard.

"Stay close. If anyone asks, we're here to visit the

deputy. Always stick as close to the truth as possible so as not to get tripped up with a lie."

"You sound like me talking to one of my students." She scanned the area, relieved that no one came out of their houses to ask questions. They might actually be able to look around without Lance finding out. Because if he was innocent, she didn't want to see the hurt expression on his face when he found out they'd suspected him.

"Let's go around back," Ryan said. "That's where we'll find a shelter or basement window."

She followed him through a chain-link gate. A few trees and a toolshed. No storm shelter, no basement window. She cupped her hands and peered through a window into a kitchen.

Spotless with flowered seat cushions on the chairs around a round table. Magnets of different states adorned the stainless-steel fridge. Places they'd traveled? "It doesn't look as if he changed anything after his wife died. Looks like it's had a woman's touch."

"Then I don't think he'd bring the women here. That would be too much like cheating. If Lance is our man, he must have another place."

"Maybe something in his wife's name? A family hunting cabin?"

"The mountain is littered with them. It's possible." He peered in another window. "Bedroom. I had no idea Bundt was such a clean freak. His desk is always cluttered."

"Let's go before someone sees us. He isn't here, and there's no sign of the hostess from last night." She shivered against a bitter winter wind.

When they were back in the car, Ryan held out his hand. "May I see your phone?"

"Yes, but why?"

"I'd like your permission to download a tracking app. While I plan on not leaving your side, I'd feel better...just in case."

Her hand trembled as she handed him her phone. Having him know where she was at every minute sounded good to her.

~

He turned onto the street just in time to see the captain's car pull away from the house. He slowed, his gaze searching the place for any sign of entry. Not seeing one, he increased his speed and followed them. Why had they gone to the house?

Rage burned through his veins. How much did they know? They couldn't have discovered his identity. It was impossible.

He slapped his hand on the side of his head. Think. Think. They had to be grasping at straws. If only they knew how close to his latest acquisition they'd come.

Convinced they were simply fishing for any minor detail they could stumble across, he pulled into a house a few doors down. A house that a had nice-sized storm shelter, built sixty years ago when some idiot thought the states would be bombed.

He unlocked the front door, locking it again behind him and headed for the stairs at the back of the kitchen. On his way down, he flipped on the light.

She lay curled up on a quilt he'd cleaned just for her. Her chains rattled as she rolled over to glare at him. "Let me go. How can you do this?"

He sat on the edge of the cot and patted her leg.

"It's really very easy, my love. I simply wrap my hands around your throat and squeeze. It's much more personal than shooting you."

Chapter Fifteen

Since Ryan wasn't officially working and had some time on his hands, he suggested they go visit Danny so the boy wouldn't feel neglected. Then, that afternoon, they'd focus more on the case. Fine with Maddy. The hour drive gave her enough time to further process the fact that Lance might be the killer.

"I spoke with Sheriff Westbrook when we returned after going to Bundt's place." Ryan's fingers tightened on the steering wheel, his knuckles turning white. "He was in and out of the office all day, presumably working the case."

"What did he say about our theory?"

"He didn't dismiss it but didn't agree either."

"Will he say something to Lance?" She swallowed against a sudden dry throat. "If he finds out we suspect—"

"He won't say anything. If Bundt is our guy, once we have the proof we need, the sheriff will present it to the feds, and they'll make the arrest."

"How do we obtain that evidence? We have to be absolutely sure. If the town finds out who we suspect and Lance turns out to be innocent, the residents will still turn against him. There will always be a shadow of distrust hanging over him." She didn't like the man; he made her uncomfortable, but she didn't want to be the reason his life fell apart if he wasn't The Abductor.

"I don't know. If I was still actively working, I could better keep an eye on him. As it is now, we're flying blind on pure speculation."

"We aren't going to know who we're really looking for until he comes for me." Her veins filled with ice.

The Abductor seemed to slip in and out of places without being seen. He took women at opportunity rather than hunting them, it seemed. Maddy should be fine as long as she stayed glued to Ryan's side. She sighed and stared out the passenger side window, wondering whether she'd actually accomplish what she'd come to Misty Hollow for. Justice for her sister. Or would she end up the same way as Alli?

Danny was ecstatic to see them and dragged both Ryan and Maddy to the room he stayed in. "Grandma and Grandpa gave me a train set that belonged to my dad." His face beamed. "Isn't it great?"

Maddy smiled at the sheer joy on his face. "You have a part of him now."

"I remember that set." Ryan stood by the table where holding the tracks. "Darren's is red, and mine was green. We tried endlessly to prove our train was the fastest."

"Who won?" Danny asked.

"The trains always went the same speed."

Grief etched lines on the sides of Ryan's mouth. Maddy moved closer, slipping her hand in his. "Maybe you and Danny can race now."

"Maybe." Ryan gave her a sad smile. "I want to

speak with my father."

"Danny and I will be fine." She watched him leave the room. "Why don't you show me how your train works?"

After fifteen minutes, Danny grew bored and headed to the kitchen for a snack, leaving Maddy to join Ryan and his father in the living room. Mrs. Maxwell entered right after she did, carrying a tray with cookies and lemonade.

"If you're going to talk of unpleasant things, at least fortify yourselves with sugar." She set the tray on the coffee table and smiled in Maddy's direction. "It's good to see you again. I hope you'll visit often when all this horror is behind us."

Since that wasn't something she could answer, Maddy simply smiled and poured each of them a glass of lemonade. "What are you two talking about?"

"I've been telling Dad about Bundt. Thanks." He accepted the glass she held out to him.

"I think it's a good assumption," Mr. Maxwell said. "The deputy would know every step of the investigation. The women he took would know him and wouldn't be frightened at first."

"How do we prove it, though?" The bite of cookie she took tasted like cardboard. Not because of Mrs. Maxwell's baking but because of the topic of conversation. She set the uneaten portion on a napkin. "Did you run across something similar during your career?"

"I've seen my share of dirty cops during my career, but none of them were serial killers." He shoved a cookie into his mouth. Obviously, the subject matter didn't hurt his appetite any. "I turned over a few to the chief myself and let him proceed."

"Staying anonymous." Ryan's lip curled. "Hard to do in a small town."

"Don't talk to me about hard, son. One of the officers I turned in was my partner of ten years. I couldn't stay anonymous then. After a short jail term, he moved out of the state. I've never heard from him." Pain laced his words. "As for proving it, all you can do is keep searching. You'll run across the evidence you need eventually."

Eventually was a long time when women were dying.

~

"Stop calling me Sarah." The pretty young thing chained to the bed glared. "Just kill me already."

"It isn't time." He paced the room, wanting very much to feel her neck between his hands. Instead, he hurried from the house, making sure it was locked up tight, and headed for his wife's car he kept closed in the garage. While he enjoyed leaving work to lay eyes on his latest prize, people would grow suspicious if he disappeared too often.

He drove the speed limit in his neighborhood, not wanting to attract unwanted attention in case the captain and Maddy returned to ask questions of the neighbors. Once he hit the exit ramp to the Interstate, he pressed the accelerator and sped toward Misty Hollow.

Well, well. He hadn't expected to see the captain and Maddy on the road. How could he get rid of Maxwell without being witnessed by Maddy or other drivers? There weren't many cars on the road, but enough that he couldn't risk running them off the road.

He drummed his fingers on the steering wheel. His

gaze fell on his gun and ski mask lying on the passenger seat. First, he slipped the mask over his head, then picked up the gun. Thankfully, he usually drove his car. Today, he'd wanted to be close to Sarah and had chosen hers. If he failed, Maxwell would be none the wiser as to his identity.

He increased his speed, easily overtaking the other vehicle and aimed his gun.

~

"Ryan!" Maddy stared wide-eyed out his window.

"Hold on." Ryan whipped the wheel sideways, slamming into the gunman's car.

The shot went wild.

Horns blared as vehicles sped past.

Hopefully, one of them would call the police. "Get your gun and return fire."

"I can't shoot past you." Maddy shook her head. "If we swerve, I could shoot you in the head."

"If you don't try, we're going to end up in the ditch." He swerved away from said ditch and increased his speed.

The gunman did the same.

"Do you recognize him?" Maddy asked. "Is it Lance?"

"He has a mask on, and I'm too busy trying not to kill us both. I can't study him right now."

The next shot sent a bolt of lightning through Ryan's shoulder. He groaned, struggling to remain upright. Spots appeared in front of his eyes. He slumped over the steering wheel, pressing the brake pedal, hoping to stop the car before he passed out.

"Ryan!"

The car careened toward the ditch.

He slammed harder on the brake, skidding to a stop, one wheel over the ditch. "Get. Down." His eyes closed.

He woke up as paramedics lifted him into the ambulance. "Maddy?"

"I'm going to follow in your car." She put a hand on his arm. "You're going to be fine."

He didn't feel fine, but seeing Maddy standing there, unharmed, was the best thing he'd seen in a very long time. On the verge of unconsciousness, he feared the worst. Feared she'd be gone, if and when, he awoke. He smiled and drifted off again.

The next time he woke up to the sight of Maddy sleeping in a chair beside his bed. His arm ached and he tried to lift it off his chest.

"You've had surgery." Maddy's eyes blinked open. "You'll have some recovery time, but the doctor said you'll regain full use of your arm."

How would he protect her with one arm in a sling? He glanced at the door as Sheriff Westbrook strolled in.

"Good to see you awake, Captain."

"Sheriff." Ryan pressed the button on the remote lying next to him and raised the bed to a sitting position.

"Bundt never showed up for work today." The sheriff sat in the chair Maddy vacated, with promises she'd return with something for Ryan to eat. "I think you might be onto something with him."

"The shooter didn't drive the same car the deputy does. I could be wrong." Or the pain meds he felt coursing through his system made his brain foggy.

"Let's not rule him out yet."

"Have you mentioned him to the feds?"

The sheriff shook his head. "Not until we have more information. I will post a guard outside your door and have a cot brought in for Miss Everton. She can't go home alone. The killer could've shot you in order to get you out of the way. Let's not make it easy for him."

Ryan agreed. His eyes drifted closed again as the sheriff stepped out of the room. Who was watching Maddy right now? He fell asleep before he had an answer.

Ryan opened his eyes later to the sound of the toilet flushing. If Maddy was in the bathroom, who was standing at the foot of his bed? He tried to wiggle into a sitting position. "Bundt?"

"You think you're clever, don't you? Do you know how easy it would be for me to kill you right now and take Maddy?" The voice sounded a bit like Bundt's, but deeper and angrier.

"Then why don't you?"

"It's not time yet. I still have my latest acquisition. Besides, I'm rather enjoying the game the three of us are playing."

The lock on the bathroom door disengaged.

The dark figure bolted from the room seconds before Maddy stepped out.

Ryan pressed the call button on his remote. "The killer was just here."

"Was it Lance?" She asked in a horrified whisper.

"I'm not sure. These meds make me loopy. Look outside and see where the guard is."

She rushed to do his bidding. "The chair is empty…oh, there he is. He'd gone to get coffee."

"Get him in here."

Miller entered the room. "You doing okay?"

"The killer was here. In my room. Next time you want a drink, ask the nurse. Need to use the restroom? Use this one." Ryan fought against the pain returning. When the nurse responded to his call, he informed her there'd be no more pain meds.

"I'll not leave my post again." Miller backed from the room.

"I'm sure the deputy thought we'd be safe in the hospital. Why didn't the man kill you?" Maddy sat and took his hand.

"Said he's enjoying the game." His gaze searched her face. "He'll be coming for you. I'm not sure I can protect you."

She lifted his hand to her cheek. "Of course, you will. You have from that night at the school. I trust you to keep doing the same."

He'd do his best as long as he drew a breath.

Chapter Sixteen

The sheriff stood on Maddy's porch, his hat in his hand. "What happened?"

"It's the third day and no sign of the hostess from Lucy's Diner, Kaye Benning. Is the captain here?"

"Of course, he is. He insisted on being released to recuperate here rather than have me stay at the hospital with him." She stepped aside to let the sheriff into the house.

"Days like the ones we're living through require sacrifice."

Maddy frowned. Maybe so, but her emotions for Ryan were all over the place, confusing her. She teetered on the line of loving him, most likely had already crossed over into love, but refused to admit it. What she would admit is that she didn't want him hurt because of her.

The sheriff stepped into the living room where Ryan lay sprawled on the sofa idly flipping through channels on the TV. Spotting his boss, he sat up, grimacing.

"Relax, Captain." The sheriff sat in the easy chair across from him.

Still able to hear their conversation, Maddy went to

make coffee. She searched the pantry for cookies—something to feed their guest but came up empty. They'd have to go to the grocery store at some point. Maybe delivery?

"Any suspicious activity from Bundt?" Ryan asked.

"He's showing up for work as he should, patrolling the streets—nothing to suggest he's anything but a deputy."

A serial-killer deputy. Maddy twisted her lips and measured the coffee grounds. She'd thought long and hard last night, and no one else came close to being the killer except for Lance.

"I'm keeping as close an eye on him as I can, even having Miller accompany him wherever he goes, which neither deputy likes very much." The sheriff exhaled heavily. "I figure if a woman disappears or a body is found while the two are together, it'll rule out Bundt as the perp."

"Makes sense," Ryan replied. "Bundt and I don't get along, but I'd hate to think he's the one behind all this."

Maddy didn't like the idea either. She poured three cups of coffee and carried them into the living room. "If it isn't Bundt, we're back at square one."

"I'll not arrest one of my men unless I'm absolutely certain." The sheriff frowned.

"I understand." She wasn't an idiot. "If you arrest the wrong man, the killings will continue."

"They might slow a bit to let the dust settle." Ryan accepted his coffee with a smile. "But, they would continue at some point. If not here, then another city. Same as this man leaving Langley and coming here."

This would never end. Maddy would have to take a big step that neither of the men in front of her would agree to. "We need to dangle me like a carrot."

"Absolutely not," they said in unison.

The sheriff stood. "I'll let you talk reason to her, Maxwell. I need to get out there and find a body. I seriously doubt he'll veer from his MO at this point."

Maddy saw the sheriff out, then squared her shoulders, ready to do battle. "It's the only way to stop him."

"He'll kill you." Ryan pushed off the sofa and stepped in front of her, his good hand curving around the back of her neck.

She fought against the urge to lean into his touch. "I have a tracker on my phone."

"Phones can be tossed."

"I'll put it down my bra."

He chuckled, leaning his forehead against hers. "I don't think that would stop him. In fact, he might like searching you. Please, see how wrong this is. How horribly dangerous."

"I know," she whispered, stepping back. "You've been shot. The next time might be fatal. I can't have him kill you."

His eyes warmed. "I feel the same about you, Madison. I…" He inhaled deeply and turned away. "We'll think of something else."

"Ryan."

He turned slowly, his gaze locking with hers, before once again moving toward her. This time, he cupped the back of her head and drew her lips to his. The kiss started tender, sweet, then grew into a fiery furnace, her passion matching his, until she knew she'd never be able to leave.

If his kiss was one of desperation or love she didn't know. All she knew was she didn't want it to end. Her arms circled his neck until her curves fell against the hard planes of his body like missing pieces of a puzzle. Neither one pulled back until they both panted for breath.

Ryan's lips curved. "No risks, okay?"

At that point she'd promise him anything. "Okay." She fought to control her breathing. "We need groceries. Shall I order delivery?"

He tilted his head, his gaze still woozy from the kiss. "I could stand to get out of the house. We can take it slow."

If he was able to kiss her like he just did, then she believed he could go shopping.

"Maddy?" His speaking her name pulled her attention back to his face. "We'll need to talk about what just happened at some point, especially if I overstepped a boundary."

A boundary? She'd given as good as she received. "It's fine. I enjoyed it." She cringed. Enjoyed it? Idiot.

He laughed. "So did I, sweetheart. So did I."

~

"Excuse me?" One of Maddy's neighbors called over her fence. "I think you would want to know that Deputy Bundt was walking around your house and peering in windows."

Ryan stiffened. "When?"

"Just a few minutes ago. He stomped away, his face all red."

"Did you see his car?"

She shook her head. "No, he took off down the

sidewalk."

He must have seen them kissing. If Bundt was The Abductor, the danger to Maddy had increased a thousand-fold. "Thank you, ma'am." He took Maddy's hand and led her to the driver's seat. "You'll have to drive."

She nodded, her face pale, and slid into the driver's seat. Ryan handed her the keys and closed the door before lowering himself into the passenger side.

"What do we do?" She asked, turning the key in the ignition.

"Wait for him to make a move." The thought scared him spitless. Again, he prayed they were wrong about the deputy. "I'll be sleeping on the sofa from now on."

"Your arm?"

"If he breaks in, whether through the front or the back, he'll have to pass by me. He'll never get to you."

By the time they'd finished shopping, fatigue coated Ryan. His bullet wound throbbed to the point he considered pain meds. No. He needed to stay alert.

They were almost to Maddy's home when the fire truck passed them, sirens blaring and lights flashing. Right behind them drove Miller and Bundt.

Bundt glanced their way and pointed ahead of them.

"Oh, dear God. Alli's house is on fire." Maddy shot a terrified look at Ryan. "It's all I have left of her." She cut another vehicle off in her haste to reach the house.

"Slow down, sweetie, or you'll get us killed." He put a hand on her leg.

She parked behind the squad car and raced for the

house. Bundt reached out and wrapped his arms around her waist.

"You can't go in there."

"Get off me." She fought until he released her and crumbled to the ground.

When Bundt reached for her again, Ryan stepped between them. "Don't touch her." He turned to Miller. "Has he been with you all day?"

"Pretty much, why?" Miller's brows rose.

"Because he was seen peeking through the window of Maddy's house an hour ago. Now, it's on fire." He glared at Bundt.

"What are you insinuating?" Bundt's fists clenched.

"It strikes me as odd. Why were you here?"

A sharp cry from Maddy as the flames shot through the roof of the house, pulled his attention away from the deputy. Ryan knelt beside her, putting his good arm around her shoulders and pulling her close. "I'm so sorry." Each sob tore at his heart.

The sheriff pulled up and strode their way. "Is she all right?"

"Yes, sir. Other than devastated anyway."

"Deputies, keep the onlookers at a safe distance. Miss Everton, we need to move you back a bit."

Ryan agreed. The heat from the flames took away the chill of the winter day. They were too close.

Maddy stood and launched herself at Bundt. "You did this! You killed Alli and now you've burned down her house." She pummeled his chest until the sheriff pulled her away.

"Control yourself, Miss Everton." He jerked his head toward the watching crowd.

Red-faced and stony-eyed, Bundt snarled and went to do crowd control.

"A neighbor saw him peeking through the windows earlier. She told us as we left to get groceries. Now, the house is burning to the ground." Ryan's blood boiled. "Too much of a coincidence."

"Is the woman positive it was our deputy?"

"She lives right next door. The houses aren't that far apart." He glanced to where the fire men doused the houses on each side of Maddy's with water.

"There's no way she was mistaken," Maddy hissed. "He's the killer, and he set fire to my house."

They'd need a place to stay, and Bundt would know the location of the nearest safehouse. "We need a place to hole up."

"Give me a few minutes to find a place." The sheriff headed to where the fire marshal waved him over.

"Come on." Ryan took Maddy's hand. He wanted to know what the marshal had discovered.

She yanked her hand free and stared at the fire that consumed what she had left of her sister. Ryan was torn between staying by her side and hearing the conversation between the marshal and the sheriff. He chose Maddy and moved to her side. No touching, just companionship during a serious loss.

The sheriff joined them, his face grave. "The body of Kaye Benning was discovered partially covered by leaves in the backyard. Find me Bundt. Now. Miss Everton, get in my car and lock the doors."

"Go on." Ryan urged her, then pulled his weapon from the holster on his hip and followed the sheriff.

They spotted Miller stringing tape to keep the

crowd back. When asked where his partner was, he pointed in the opposite direction. "Said he would put up the tape at that end."

~

The gig was up. The stupid hag had seen him running from Maddy's house. Oh, he'd returned and dumped the pretty little Kaye, and now he wanted to rid the world of the nosy neighbor, but he constrained himself.

Miller asked too many question when Lance was late. When he'd returned after seeing Maddy and Ryan in a lip-lock, the other deputy had picked up on the anger radiating from him. He'd waved it off to traffic on the Interstate, not sure the other man had bought the excuse.

Three days or not, he wouldn't take another woman until he could grab Maddy. The risk was too high. He'd snatch and run, leaving everything behind and forge a new life in another state. Maybe a new country. He knew where he could obtain new identities for them both.

He could forgive her for her moment of weakness in kissing the captain. After all, they'd been thrust together by circumstances caused by Lance. The kiss had been entirely his fault. No worries. Maddy would come to love him soon enough.

Lance jumped in his car and sped toward home. He needed to hide his car and drive Sarah's before the sheriff could put an APB out on him. When that happened and the news found out, the townspeople would come out in droves like vigilantes.

So many things to do. The room where Kaye had been kept needed to be cleaned. Food needed to be ordered and delivered. Plans needed to be made.

The sheriff would send them somewhere he deemed safe, but Lance knew all the places people could hide. Misty Hollow had several rental properties, and he'd checked them all out, going so far as to install tiny cameras. He'd know when someone moved in. The captain wouldn't take the chance of staying at a hotel. They'd want privacy.

Then, when he saw her again, he'd take her.

Chapter Seventeen

The ringing of Maddy's phone woke her. "Hello?"

"It's…Susan." Her words broke on a sob.

Maddy sat upright, waving to Ryan in the other bed that everything was fine. "Are you okay?"

"I'm back in Misty Hollow."

"Why?" It was too dangerous. More so now that no one knew where Lance was.

"Funeral for my cousin, Kaye. I couldn't stay away." She sniffed. "I tried to convince her to leave, I really did, but she insisted on staying for her job. I should have tried harder."

"You did what you could. I'm so sorry." Maddy's throat clogged.

"You have to leave there. I'm headed out again right after the funeral in a couple of days."

"We're closing in on catching him. Now is not the time for me to run." Although, she was mighty tempted considering who the killer turned out to be. Lance—someone she'd gone out to dinner with—the thought made her shudder. "I'm staying with Captain Maxwell. I'll be fine."

"Please be careful."

Maddy promised and returned her phone to the nightstand. "That was Susan Snodgrass. Lance's latest victim was her cousin. She's here for the funeral."

"The body hasn't been released yet."

"What does that mean?" She rolled onto her side, barely able to make out his shape on the other bed in the dark.

"It means she's here too early."

Maddy's heart skipped a beat. "Lured here?"

"Maybe. I need to call the sheriff." He reached for his phone. "I'm not putting anything past Lance at this point."

Maddy lay there and listened while he discussed her phone call with the sheriff. Why would Lance lure Susan back to Misty Hollow if it was Maddy he wanted? They were making quite the assumption. She could have returned due to a misunderstanding on the dates. Maybe she'd only been told about Kaye's murder and assumed the funeral would be soon. It wasn't too far-fetched of an idea.

"Call Susan back. The sheriff wants to know why she thinks the funeral is close." Ryan's request broke through her thoughts.

When Susan answered, Maddy put her on speaker and asked, "Who told you about the funeral?"

"My cousin, Ted."

"Are you sure it was Ted?"

"Well, I haven't seen or spoken to him in years. Why would he lie? What's this about?"

"Miss Snodgrass, this is Captain Maxwell. We believe you were led back to suffer the same fate as Kaye. The killer is Deputy Lance Bundt. The FBI are sending someone to escort you to a safe place. Do you understand?"

She gasped. "I'm such a fool."

"No." Maddy wanted to reach out and touch her. "You're grieving. You'll believe anything a family member tells you. It's possible Bundt called you. This is only a precaution." She met Ryan's gaze who nodded.

"The sheriff's department will be in touch with your cousin, Ted. If he is the one who called you, you'll be free to return to where you were," Ryan said. "If it wasn't him, you'll stay under guard until Bundt is captured. Make sure the agent that shows up at your door shows ID. It will be either Agent Starling or Agent Lee."

"Okay." Her voice shook. "Can I go now?"

"Yes, ma'am. Stay safe." Ryan reached over and pressed the button on Maddy's phone. "I think Bundt is tying up loose ends. Which means, Susan saw something, or he believes she did, and isn't taking any chances of her remembering whatever it is."

She shook her head and lay back on her pillow. "It's me he wants. Time for him to leave the other women alone." He'd killed too many.

"Go to sleep, Maddy. I'll keep watch." Ryan moved to her side and leaned down, planting a tender kiss on her forehead before heading to the bathroom.

Maddy smiled and snuggled deeper under the covers knowing he'd do everything in his power to keep the promise he'd whispered. She said a prayer for Susan's safety and closed her eyes.

The rattling of the bathroom doorknob and pounding on the door woke her. She blinked through the dark to see a shadow at the foot of her bed. "Ryan?"

"Maddy!"

She glanced from the shadow to the bathroom where a rod held the door closed, then lunged for the gun on her nightstand.

Lance's hand closed around her wrist. His teeth glowed in what little light there was in the room. "Finally," he spoke on an exhale of breath.

The bathroom door banged open, and Ryan fell out.

Maddy clutched her gun.

Lance whipped around and dove through the front window, glass shattering as Maddy's shot rang out.

"Stay here." Ryan grabbed his gun from his nightstand and gave chase, using the door instead of the window.

Maddy kept one hand on the butt of her gun, the other pulling the blanket to her chin. What if Lance lured Ryan out so he could circle back around and get her? She whispered Ryan's name in the dark as sirens wailed, growing closer.

~

So close. How did Maxwell break open the door with only one good shoulder? He cursed and raced across the highway, narrowly missing getting run over by a semi. A glance over his shoulder spurred him on.

"Stop." Maxwell gave chase, lumbering like a misshapen beast as he held his wounded shoulder close to his side.

Lance wanted to pause long enough to fire a shot, but slowing would increase his chance of capture. He had no doubt he could outrun the captain since he wasn't injured.

Sirens rose, growing closer. He should've known

the house would have security cameras. The authorities had been alerted the instant he'd entered the small house once owned by Miller's grandmother. Had they really thought Lance wouldn't know about the house?

He'd almost outsmarted them. Was he losing his touch? No. Ryan was the reason he didn't have Maddy yet. The other women hadn't had law enforcement sleeping in the same room or even the same house. They hadn't had someone escorting them from here to there. They'd been easy pickings. Having Maxwell so close to Maddy only made the hunt more of a challenge.

A shot rang out. Lance swerved, changed directions, and hopped over a small hill into a creek bed. The frigid, fast-moving water took his breath away as it carried him out of Maxwell's reach.

~

Ryan stood on the rise and watched the former deputy disappear out of sight, carried by the swift water of the creek. He'd taken a shot when the clouds parted, letting the moon light the way, and missed. His teeth chattered and he rubbed his arms, having rushed out in nothing more than a tee shirt and thin flannel bottoms. His feet ached from running over rocks and rough ground.

He'd have another chance at Bundt. Ryan glanced at the mud at the edge of the creek, spotting the same print he'd found outside Maddy's window. Unfortunately, he didn't have his phone with him.

By the time he limped back to the house that hadn't been safe after all, emergency vehicle lights lit up the night. Inside, Maddy sat on the sofa being questioned by Starling.

The sheriff took one look at Ryan's feet and demanded a paramedic examine them.

Ryan endured the medic's attention when what he really wanted was to make sure Maddy was okay. She looked fine, a bit shaken up, but Bundt had actually had his hand on her.

"Minor abrasions. I'd wear socks for a while to keep the scrapes clean." The medic stood. "Walking will feel tender for a few days."

"Thanks. I'll be all right." Ryan hopped from the back of the ambulance, winced at the pain in his feet, and limped to where Maddy sat.

"I see he got away," Starling said, her eyes hard.

"Couldn't quite catch him with a gunshot in one shoulder and no shoes on my feet. Bundt jumped into the creek on the other side of the highway and was swept away. I doubt we'd be lucky enough to find his body along the shore." He took Maddy's hands in his. "Okay?"

She nodded. "Worried about you the whole time. I wondered whether Lance was going to circle back. Oh, I had plenty to occupy my mind while you were gone." She forced a smile.

Chuckling, he pulled her under his good arm and glanced back at the sheriff. "What else do you want to know? It was definitely Bundt. No question that he's the killer."

"There's an APB out on him, and the news is flashing his photo every hour. Hopefully, someone knows where he's hiding out. A neighbor, maybe." He checked his phone.

"When we visited the address in his file, we couldn't find any sign that he'd kept any of the women there. The place was spotless."

"I'll check it out. Do some knocking on doors. Looks like you're on medical leave now, instead of guard duty."

Ryan rotated his shoulder. "I can do both." There's no way he'd stop watching over Maddy.

The sheriff scratched his chin, then nodded. "I'll let you know what I find out."

"There's a print by the creek. Same one I found outside Maddy's window that time. More proof if you want to send someone to take a photo." He leaned his head against the back of the sofa, exhausted. "I can show you if you want."

"No need," Agent Lee said, entering the room. "I'll find it. I'm sure the two of you left plenty of tracks for me to follow once the sun comes up."

"Where do we go now?" Maddy stayed against Ryan's side.

"I don't know. We can't keep house-hopping. It has to be somewhere with absolutely no ties to anyone in the department." He hadn't been in Misty Hollow long enough to know of such a place.

"I'll ask around. For now, a hotel is your best bet." The sheriff turned and left, the feds following him from the house.

Misty Hollow didn't have one. Ryan sighed. "Let's gather up our things. I'll find us a place to crash, even if it's a shack on the mountain." Which might not be a bad idea. There were a lot of hunting cabins up there. It'd be harder for Bundt to find them.

Once they were dressed and their few belongings in the trunk of his car, he headed up the mountain. Ryan would look for a road that didn't look well-traveled and hope to find a decent cabin that sat empty. No need to be greeted by a shotgun.

"Where are we going?" Maddy glanced around.

"I'm not sure yet. I'll find something. Why not grab some sleep?"

"No. You might need me to help you stay awake. We can't use someone's cabin without permission, can we?"

"I'll leave compensation. We can't sleep in the car or we'll freeze." Not that any of the cabins up there had electricity. He could only hope for a stack of firewood. Ryan reached for Maddy's hand. "Don't worry. I'll take care of you."

"I know." She gave his hand a squeeze. "I trust you more than I've trusted anyone other than my parents and Alli."

Her words filled him with pleasure. Gone was his resolve to focus on his career and Danny. The future held the promise of Maddy. Danny needed a mother figure in his life. Someone to help him deal with the violent loss of his parents.

He turned left onto a road, drove past a well-maintained cabin he knew belonged to Spencer Thorne, ex-military man who liked living off the grid as much as possible. They'd met once at the diner, along with his lovely wife, Sierra.

As he drove further, the road became rougher, finally emerging into an overgrown clearing where a small cabin stood. The rising sun pointed out its flaws, the sagging porch, the leaning chimney, but it was a roof over their head.

Bundt wouldn't suspect they'd stay in such a place. He hoped.

CYNTHIA HICKEY

Chapter Eighteen

Ryan stepped onto the cabin's lopsided porch to answer the sheriff's call. Seeing Maddy curled up in a tattered sleeping bag, he didn't have the heart to wake her.

"Maxwell."

"The address Bundt used on his employment record is false," the sheriff said. "According to the neighbors, he lives two doors down from that house."

Ryan leaned against a fence post, hoping it wouldn't fall from under him. "Did you search the place?"

"Sure did. Found a cellar with a room containing a bed, a toilet, and a bolt in the wall with chains. The perfect cell to hold a woman captive. No one would be able to hear her scream."

"Any idea where he might be now? Relatives?"

"Nada. Be careful up there. He could be staying close, and you wouldn't know until he was right on top of you."

True. A man with a rifle stepped from the trees. "Hold on, Sheriff. Someone is here."

"Don't hang up."

Ryan stepped off the porch, one hand on the gun at

his hip. "State your purpose here."

The man grinned. "I could say the same to you, Captain." He thrust out his hand. "Spencer Thorne. You passed my place on your way here. Mind telling me why you're here?"

"It's all good," he told the sheriff before hanging up. He returned his attention to Thorne. "Sheriff's business. You own this place?"

He shook his head. "The man who did died a while back. His offspring could care less about this cabin. This place is cursed, some say."

"Why?" Ryan didn't believe in such things.

"Last year, my wife's brother stayed here."

"So?" Ryan frowned.

"He hid here hoping to find the right time to grab my wife and run." His gaze flicked to Ryan's shoulder. "Looks like you've had your share of trouble. Mind if I sit?"

Ryan glanced toward the door, half expecting to see Maddy come out, and glad she didn't. Until he knew whether he could trust this man, he preferred she stay hidden. "Make yourself at home." Ryan sat on the top step, Thorne sitting one below him.

He leaned his rifle against the railing. "I saw the smoke which is how I knew you were here. This isn't much of a cabin. Roof leaks and the chinking between the logs is gone in a lot of places. You hiding from someone?"

"Maybe."

"Look, I've been in your shoes. Hid out with Sierra my share of times trying to keep her out of her brother's clutches. I don't got a lot of room, but if you and the teacher want to stay with us, you'll be safer. Two guns are better than one, after all."

"Make that three." A tousled-headed Maddy stood in the doorway. "How did you know about me?"

"Everyone in town knows about you getting attacked at the school."

Ryan exhaled heavily as she joined them. The more the man talked, the more Ryan remembered hearing about this man's wife's case last year. The sheriff seemed to think highly of him. "I guess you've heard about the identity of The Abductor by now?"

"No TV."

"Deputy Bundt." Maddy crossed her arms.

Thorne's eyes widened. "Wouldn't have guessed that one."

"Took us by surprise." Ryan glanced at Maddy. "What do you want to do?"

"I'd hate to bring danger to their doorstep."

"Sierra and I both know how to shoot. Like I said, there's strength in numbers. Why don't the two of you think it over and let me know? I bet you don't have food, water, or coffee. Am I right?"

"You'd be right." Ryan said. He'd planned on leaving Maddy there while he ran into town. It'd be safe for a day or two, before Bundt stumbled upon the place.

"Come on. At least have breakfast and coffee. Sierra is already planning on you coming." Thorne stood.

Ryan peered at Maddy who nodded. "All right. Coffee and breakfast do sound pretty good."

They drove to Thorne's house rather than walked. If Ryan did decide to stay in the dilapidated cabin, he'd still need to drive into town for supplies. Not to mention walking on his injured feet which wasn't something he looked forward to.

A pretty woman with hair a lighter shade of blond than Maddy's stood on the porch. "Your wife is blond," Maddy said. "Weren't you worried for her?"

"She hasn't left this cabin in days." Thorne led the way to the cabin. "Sierra, Captain Maxwell and Miss Everton."

"Please, it's Maddy."

"And Ryan. Glad to meet you, ma'am."

"Come in. I've eggs, bacon, and sausage with biscuits and gravy. I didn't know what you liked so cooked a bit of everything. Don't mind the dogs. They like to stay underfoot when we're eating." She ushered them inside the tastefully decorated cabin.

"Thank you." Maddy took a seat, Ryan sitting next to her at the table for four. "I've seen you at the coffee shop."

"I work there." Sierra's gaze flicked to her husband. "Spencer insisted I take time off until The Abductor is caught."

"Your husband is wise to do so." Ryan chose biscuits with thick white gravy and bacon. His stomach rumbled at the delicious aromas coming from the food. He sat back as Maddy cut his food for him, feeling a bit foolish that his left arm was useless, and he had to be waited on like a toddler. "It's been all I can handle to keep Maddy out of the killer's clutches."

~

The talk around the table switched from Maddy's ordeal to Sierra's the year before. "You can imagine how I felt finding out the man I was going to marry was actually my half-brother. I can't believe my mother kept such a secret."

"You were planning on breaking up with him anyway," Spencer said, lifting a coffee cup to his lips.

"Yes, because he'd changed. If he hadn't developed the brain tumor, I would have married him." She shuddered. "How awful that would have been. Anyway, the tumor kept him from seeing reason, and he grew obsessed with me."

"Like Bundt has with Maddy." Ryan glanced around the table. "Didn't the sheriff have something like this happen with his wife? Seems I read something in a newspaper."

Thorne nodded. "His wife took a DNA test, which led to her discovering that she and her mother had come to Misty Hollow in the witness protection program to escape her biological father, Anthony Bartelloni, the crime boss."

"Misty Hollow has had its share of troubles." Ryan shook his head.

"Yep. Thankfully, the events haven't been back-to-back. There's crime everywhere, Captain. You know that. Even in small towns."

"I do know."

"So, what about our offer of staying here? The sofa pulls out into a bed."

Ryan glanced at Maddy. "Your decision."

"Hmm." She was still hesitant about bringing Bundt to their doorstep, especially after finding out Sierra was a blonde. "Can we let you know by the end of the day?"

"Sure. But, if you stay in that cabin again tonight, at least let us lend you proper sleeping bags and blankets."

She smiled. "That we can do." Before making a decision that could affect other people's lives, she wanted to visit the lake. Although Alli's body had been dumped there, she hadn't lost her life there. The beautiful scenery and calm surface of the water soothed Maddy and helped her think. It was the only place she felt close to her sister now.

After she helped Sierra clean up after breakfast, she motioned Ryan to join her outside and mentioned the idea to him. "Do you mind?"

"Are you sure?" His brow furrowed. "Going into town could be dangerous."

"I really need to go there." She took his hand. "I know standing on your feet is painful. There's a bench not too far away that you can sit on and still see me."

His gaze caressed her face. "I don't want anything to happen to you." He cupped her cheek. "I couldn't bear it."

"You'll be right there." She smiled, leaning into his touch.

He leaned down, pressing his lips softly against hers. "Anything you want. Promise to stay in my sight."

A little over half an hour later, Maddy stood on the dock, bright yellow leaves clutched in her hand. Silk ones this time since the trees had long lost their foliage. She glanced back to see Ryan settling on the bench and waved before staring at the calm surface of the water. Water that had washed her sister up until she'd floated against the dock's pilings.

Maddy dropped the leaves in the water, the action causing ripples to spread. "Oh, Alli. We've found your killer. Did you smile at him when he came for you? Did you know Lance? I pray your death was quick."

Although just like the others, her sister had suffered for three days only to be strangled at the end.

"The world isn't as bright a place without you in it." Tears blurred her vision. "But I do think I'm in love. I think he feels the same. The problem is…I don't want to stay in Misty Hollow. You aren't buried here. The ashes I scattered over this lake will have floated away. This town holds only sadness for me. Do you think Ryan would be willing to move for me?" She sat cross-legged on the weathered wood and let the tears fall.

"I guess I shouldn't worry about that yet. The fear over facing Lance is about all I can deal with. That and worrying something will happen to Ryan. He's been shot already. His shoulders slump with exhaustion when he thinks I'm not looking. He limps on wounded feet." She glanced back again to see Ryan, his good hand dangling between his legs, as he watched a group of teenage boys on skateboards.

"I've done nothing but bring destruction and pain to him. He even sent his nephew away because of me. Oh, Alli." She covered her face with her hands. "I wish you were here to talk to me."

Maddy stared again at the water, the leaves halfway across the lake, drifting to the other shore. Just like her sister's ashes had done the first day she'd arrived and the yellow leaves every day since she'd let them filter through her fingers. She sat there, the winter sun warm on her back, and let memory after memory float through her mind. Times when they were children and their parents were still alive. Now, Maddy was the only one left. If she didn't stay in Misty Hollow, if she walked away from Ryan, she'd be truly alone.

Life could be unfair. She pushed to her feet and stared heavenward. "Until I see you again, Allison."

She wiped her eyes on the sleeve of her sweater and moved to the bench where Ryan sat. He smiled up at her. "Ready to go?"

"In a bit." She sat next to him. "It's such a nice day. I'd like to pretend Lance doesn't want to kill me and that we're enjoying the sunshine."

"Sounds good to me." He put his good arm along the back of the bench. "Having a normal day is exactly what we need."

She leaned her head against his shoulder, determined to enjoy his presence for as long as she could.

Until a scream ripped through the peaceful day.

Chapter Nineteen

Ryan lunged to his feet and started to dart toward the sound only to stop and glance back at Maddy. Clearly torn between wanting to go help and stay with her, he froze.

"Go." She waved a hand. "It's your job. I'll stay right here for a few minutes, then follow you."

"Come with me now." He held out his hand.

"No, I'll just be in the way." It might be dangerous. She couldn't be a distraction. "Go," she said, when the scream came again.

Mouth set in a grim line, he rushed toward the screams coming from around the bend of the sidewalk.

Maddy sat, her hands clenched so hard together her knuckles ached. Gone was the warmth of the day. Now a bitter cold brought a shiver that had nothing to do with the weather. She took in the whole area. Five minutes, she'd give Ryan. If she didn't hear another scream or a gunshot and he hadn't returned, she'd go in search of him.

Shouts and the sound of a scuffle reached her ears. Did Ryan need her help? No, she could hear him telling someone to stop. Her heart rate slowed a bit. Sounded like a group of kids causing mischief. At least she hoped so.

She stood.

A hand clamped around her arm.

Something hard poked her back.

"Come with me, Darlin'. Don't make me kill the captain." Lance's breath tickled the hair behind her ears.

Her heart lodged in her throat. "You caused something to get him away from me."

"Clever, wasn't it? The things a group of teenagers will do for a few bucks." His grip on her arm tightened. "Hurry now. We've a ways to go."

"Everyone will be looking for us."

"Good for them. I like a challenge. Walk as if you're happy to see me."

Maddy wasn't an actress, but she did her best to keep her face passive, avoiding eye contact with most of the people they passed. The last thing she wanted was an innocent bystander shot. She knew the gesture to signal for help. When they strolled past a park ranger, she held her fingers wide, then closed her fist over her thumb. Hopefully, the man knew what the gesture meant.

With a slight nod, he reached for the radio on his belt.

Maddy's heart slowed a bit. Come on, Ryan. Find us before he forces me into a vehicle.

They approached the same car driven by the man who'd shot Ryan. "It was you."

"In the front seat." He aimed the gun at her stomach.

She scrambled into the car, wishing she'd had a chance to move her cell phone from her pocket to her bra. Lance was bound to take it from her.

He slid in the driver's seat and set his gun in his lap before starting the car. "Seatbelt. Wouldn't want you injured if we get into an accident."

"Why are you doing this?" She clicked her seatbelt into place.

"Because we're meant to be together. Shh. Everything will be fine. Hand me your phone." He held out his hand.

Her hopes fell as she dug it from her pocket and dropped it into his hand. He tossed it out the window as the park ranger drove into sight.

Lance pressed the accelerator, spinning gravel as he sped away from the lake. "Can't take any chances, can we?"

Ryan would never find her without her tracker. Her hands trembled in her lap. She had three days to find a way to escape. No, he would kill her on the third day, which left today and tomorrow, or she'd be dumped like her sister and the others. It didn't seem like enough time. Not nearly enough.

"Don't worry. Everything will be just fine." Lance tossed her a smile. "You're so much like her, you know. Sarah. I thought Allison would be the perfect replacement, but I was mistaken. You are perfect right down to the hair length and color."

"Don't you dare speak my sister's name."

"Still raw?" His brows rose. "Okay. I won't mention her again." He patted her knee, making her skin crawl.

She scooted as close to the door as possible. Maybe it would fly open, and she'd fall out. She'd rather take her chances rolling down the road than with a man as nuts as Lance. With one hand, she reached for the door. The other inched toward the release button on her seatbelt.

"If you do that, I'll turn the car around, run over you, then go kill Maxwell. Your choice." Lance kept his gaze on the road ahead of them. A vein bulged in his neck.

Maddy moved her hands back to her lap. Angering the man wouldn't work in her favor. Her mind whirled. There had to be a way to keep him from killing her.

"How much farther?"

He cut her a glance without moving his head. "Anxious? That's good. It isn't much, but it's only temporary. I'll find us a much nicer place to settle." He made a move to touch her again.

She shrank back.

His eyes flashed, and his face darkened. With a huff, he turned on the radio to a country music station.

The rest of the drive was spent in silence except for the cheating lovers in twangy lyrics. Maddy breathed a sigh of relief when they pulled up in front of a small red-brick house in the town of Forestville.

"Let's get started." Lance grinned at her.

Her blood ran cold.

~

Ryan stood in the gravel parking lot of the lake and stared in horror at Maddy's cell phone. When the park ranger had called the sheriff who then called Ryan, he didn't think his heart could drop further. But, it did.

"We'll find her," the sheriff said. "This time we know who has her."

"He lured me away by paying a group of punk kids to cause a distraction. He's smarter than we are."

"No, he isn't, and Miss Everton is smarter than he is. The other women trusted a deputy. It's different this time. Maddy won't trust him for a second."

That was true but did little to ease the anxiety coursing through him. "Someone get a print of the tire tracks."

"The car was an older model Oldsmobile, golden brown, pristine condition," the park ranger said. "I took a photo of the license plate as they sped off. The dust obscured one of the letters, but it ought to help." He showed Ryan his phone.

Local plates. He jotted down the numbers while the sheriff called them in to find out who owned the car.

"Also, find out everything you can on Lance Bundt. Dead relatives, family real estate holdings...I know you have been. Move faster!" The sheriff jammed a finger at the off button. "Here come the feds. Always fashionably late."

Ryan glared as Starling and Lee approached them. "You're here to catch this guy. Why haven't you? Did the agency send its most incompetent agents because we're a small, mountain town?" He snarled and stormed to the water's edge.

Waiting for information was the hardest part. Not knowing the next move, where to start, came in a close second. He had less than two days to find Maddy. When he did, he'd tell her exactly how he felt about her. Hopefully, she'd feel the same.

His feet ached from standing, but he didn't sit on the nearby bench. The pain kept him alert. Why should he sit in comfort when Maddy was going through who knew what?

Pressure built under his ribcage like a fist pressing

hard, trying to reach his spine. He took deep breaths through his nose and out his mouth, feeling as helpless as he had when he'd received the call about his brother's and sister-in-law's murder.

Sheriff Westbrook stood beside him, not saying anything.

Ryan appreciated the man's attempt to offer comfort, but nothing would be right again until Maddy returned alive. He squared his shoulders and watched a mallard duck swim across the lake's surface.

"Looks like glass, doesn't it?" Sheriff Westbrook asked after several minutes of silence. "Looked just like this the day we found Allison Everton. We will not find Madison's body. We'll find her alive."

"How do you know that?" Ryan gritted his teeth.

"I was a fed once. Came to Misty Hollow as an undercover sheriff. I knew who she and her mother were. I even lent my services to her father when Karlie went to face him. Offered myself as a bodyguard. Karlie ended up being the one to save me."

"What does this have to do with Maddy?" Ryan growled.

"Because she's going to find a way free. Our women are like that. With or without our help, they find a way to persevere. Madison is no different than Karlie or Spencer Thorne's wife."

Ryan grabbed onto the promise with every fiber of his being. He had to trust Maddy to know what to do. She'd gone on a date with Bundt. Been around him a few times. He wasn't a complete stranger to her. Maddy would find a way out. "So, we wait."

"Yes." The sheriff turned and headed for his car. "Go home, Captain. I'll call you as soon as I know something."

How could Ryan simply return to an empty house? Maddy's home was gone, Danny was with his grandparents, so there was no reason not to return to his own home other than the two people he cared the most about in the world weren't there. He marched to his car and drove to the nearest motel, stopping at a gas station for a sandwich and a bottle of water.

In his rented room, he set his gun and phone on the nightstand. Maddy's had been taken as evidence. Not that they needed it for fingerprints. They knew Lance had her. How had Ryan worked with the man and not have sensed the evil in him?

He fell onto the mattress and toed off his shoes, breathing an audible sigh of relief at freeing his feet. Whether he wanted to or not, he needed rest if he was going to be any good to Maddy at all.

~

"You don't have to tie me up," Maddy said, stepping back. "I'm not going anywhere. Where could I go without a car?"

"I need to know you can't." He held up a roll of duct tape. "I won't do your feet unless you force me to. You'll have a lot of freedom. You can reach the sink and the toilet. The cot is quite comfortable, although it gets a little chilly at night. If you're good, I can bring you an electric heater."

"If I'm good?" Her eyes widened. "I'm not a child, Lance."

"I know that. Now, hold out your hands. I don't want to fight with you."

She slowly lifted her hands.

He wound the tape around her wrists. "See? That's

161

not so bad. You can even lift the glass to your mouth if you're thirsty."

She plopped onto the cot and glared up at him, then shook her head and turned away, shoulders sagging.

It impressed him that she didn't cry or beg, reinforcing the fact she was the one he should've taken a long time ago. But, the hunger to kill nagged at him. It wouldn't be her, though. He'd find someone else. A homeless person, maybe, now that his search for Sarah's replacement was ended. All he needed was to feel the life force leave someone as he strangled them.

"What do you want from me, Lance?" She asked softly.

"Your love. The others couldn't give me what only you can."

Chapter Twenty

Clutching Maddy's arm, Lance led/pulled/pushed her into the house. She wanted to cooperate so she wouldn't anger him, but the closer they got to the front door, the more she dragged her feet.

Now, she stood in a living room straight out of the 1970s, complete with an orange sofa picturing a forest scene with deer, and a green shag carpet. Through an archway, she spotted the corner of an autumn gold refrigerator. "Whose house is this?"

"It belonged to my grandmother. It's mine now, although I don't live here. It's listed for sale, but no one seems to want to renovate. Sit." He shoved her onto the sofa and disappeared down the hall.

Maddy stared at the front door, then at her hands taped in her lap. Why had he left her with a means of escape? Having her hands in front of her allowed for some usage. She stood and glanced the way he'd gone.

If she was dealing with one of her students, she'd think this was a test of some kind. Should she move toward the door to find out?

The sound of approaching, muffled footsteps had her back on the sofa. Lance smiled. "Are you hungry?

Thirsty? I could fix you something."

"I'd like my hands free."

"Not yet." His smile widened as he headed for the kitchen. "Go ahead and look around. I'll be taking you downstairs in a bit. Can't chance anyone seeing you."

"The nearest neighbor is half a mile away." Maddy moved to the fireplace mantel where photos of Lance as a little boy filled the space. Cute. Who knew he'd grow up to become a serial murderer? If his grandmother was like most, it'd break her heart to know what Lance had become.

"Here." He slung a crocheted bag around her neck. "Your food and water for the next few days."

"Where are you going to be?" She widened her eyes.

"Around." His smile didn't quite reach his eyes. "I've a place in the basement ready for you."

"How sweet." She smirked and stumbled as he shoved her toward what she'd thought would be a closet but was instead the door to the basement.

A long set of wooden stairs led to a dirt floor. Several piles of boxes made a room of sorts around a cot, a portable toilet, and a shelf. Maddy supposed that was where she was to put the supplies he'd given her.

"The boxes aren't perfect walls, but don't worry. I'll announce myself when I come visit in case, well, you know." He jerked his head toward the toilet.

She muttered again, "How sweet," and exhaled heavily. So this was where she'd spend the next two days before meeting her end.

"I spent time down here with my grandmother during a tornado warning." Lance perched on a three-legged stool. "I'm glad to be back here with you."

"Is this where you brought the others?" She swallowed back her fear and met his gaze as if her insides weren't slowly turning to lead.

"Oh, no. None of them were special enough to come to my grandmother's house." His brow lowered. "This is just for you."

She didn't want to be special to him. She wanted Alli back. She wanted to see Ryan. She wanted to go home.

Lance removed the bag from around her neck and dropped it on the cot. "I should be here three times a day if not more but wanted you taken care of in case I got held up."

"You're leaving now?"

He nodded. "I should be back by dark if not shortly after. Don't worry." He patted her knee and climbed the stairs, pausing at the top. "Get some sleep. That way, you won't be tired when I come to spend time with you. It's time we took things to the next level, don't you think?"

Hopefully, she'd be gone by then. "I am tired." She forced a smile, deciding not to acknowledge his remark about the next level, then dropped to her knees beside the cot the instant the basement door closed.

Out of sight in case the door opened again, she brought her hands up, then slashed them down and apart to rip the tape from her hands. She wadded up the tape and shoved it under the cot before sneaking up the stairs. Her hand gripped the knob. She slowly turned. Locked.

Okay, Madison, think. He'll be back. Most likely in two to three hours. What she needed was a weapon. She wasn't sure whether the next level was death or…something intimate? She shuddered.

After rummaging in the boxes and finding nothing but decades of magazines and newspapers, she rushed to the other side of the room. Didn't most people keep tools in the basement? A hammer?

The winter chill seeped through the walls as the day neared its end. Maddy's breath wafted from her mouth like a soft whisper. She'd freeze to death before she had to worry about Lance wrapping his hands around her throat.

Desperate to find something, she started digging in the dirt floor with her hands. Worst case scenario, she could knock a stack of boxes on top of Lance, but that wouldn't stop him for long.

A fingernail broke at the quick. Maddy hissed at the pain but kept searching in the dirt for something. Her breath caught as her fingers curled around a nail as long as her hand. She didn't know why anyone would need a nail of that size, but it provided her with exactly what she needed.

A weapon that could be easily concealed.

~

Lance sat outside the movie theater. Somewhere in there was the woman he'd take tonight. No more three days, though. Unfortunately, he'd have to take them deep into the woods. Then, he'd feed his hunger before returning to Maddy.

So far, she'd behaved. His heart rate increased. Could it be he'd finally found someone to replace Sarah? A wife to come home to at the end of the day? Someone to love and be loved in return?

The fact she'd remained on the sofa rather than trying to bolt out the front door had reaffirmed to him that Maddy was the one. She wouldn't have gotten far if she'd tried to run, but the fact she hadn't made the attempt filled him with hope.

He straightened as three women who looked to be in their mid-twenties talked and giggled as they crossed the parking lot toward their cars. His eyes zoned in on the blonde getting into a white Camry. Nice. They'd all driven separately.

He followed her to a gated community where she punched in a code, and a large gate swung open. A car between Lance and his prey cut him off, keeping him from being able to enter.

He cursed and slammed the palm of his hand against the steering wheel. The sun had now fully set, but he didn't want to return until he'd satisfied his hunger. He turned around and headed for the nearest grocery store.

~

"The car from the lake with Madison inside is owned by a Mrs. Lambert, a widow on the north side of town." The sheriff plopped a printed photo of an elderly woman's driver's license on the desk in front of Ryan. "Reported the car stolen yesterday."

Ryan stared at the gray-haired woman. "Where was the car taken from?"

"Grocery store."

"Let's go see whether anyone saw anything." A long shot but better than sitting around waiting for information to come to him.

In his car, he asked, "What exactly are the feds doing in regard to Maddy's abduction?"

"Knocking on doors and asking questions." Sheriff Westbrook shook his head. "A waste of time since she was taken from the lake. No houses there, and the only witness was the ranger. They have to follow protocol. I do too, but Bundt has been at large for too long. Time to step away from the rules."

Ryan couldn't agree more. He drove slowly around the parking lot of the grocery store in Langley where the car had been stolen. "There it is." He parked behind the stolen car. "He has to be inside." Where was Maddy? Ryan doubted Bundt would have brought her with him. "I think he's hunting."

"Why?" The sheriff frowned. "He has the one he wants."

"Lance is insane. He can't help himself. With or without Maddy, he'll keep killing." Ryan gripped the steering wheel.

"Are you saying you think he won't kill Maddy?" The sheriff turned to face him. "That goes against his MO."

"I know, but what if she pretends to love him? To do what he says, what he wants. If his wife's death triggered his killing spree, and Maddy can convince him she's capable of stepping into his wife's shoes…it's far-fetched for sure."

The sheriff shrugged. "Stranger things have happened. Let's check out the store. Try to find out whether anyone else is missing a vehicle. He could have traded."

Which made more sense than a wanted man wandering the food aisles in search of his next victim. Bundt wasn't that stupid. "You go inside, I'll keep watch out here."

Sheriff Westbrook nodded and pushed open the glass door. "Keep your radio handy. If he's cornered, he won't care who gets between him and freedom."

Freedom wasn't something Bundt would ever have. He'd either be behind bars soon or on the run for the rest of his life. His heart skipped a beat at the thought that he might take Maddy on the run with him.

Ryan watched every person who entered or exited the store. Scanned the parking lot over and over. No one seemed frightened or anxious. A couple of blond women drove away. That alone told him Bundt was no longer around.

A middle-aged couple exited the store and froze in the middle of the parking lot, looking this way and that. "I know I parked it right there," he said.

"It's not as if the camper doesn't stick out like a sore thumb," the woman said. "Whoever took it, took the jeep, too." She leaned into the man.

"Excuse me. I'm Captain Maxwell of the Misty Hollow sheriff's department. Are you missing something?"

"Yes, sir. Our camper and jeep. We parked the camper at that end of the lot with the jeep on a trailer."

"Did you leave the keys inside?"

The man shoved his hand into his pocket and retrieved a key ring with several keys dangling from it. "Nope. Have them right here."

Bundt had just given himself a home on wheels. Unfortunate for him, campers weren't as easily hidden as a car.

The sheriff joined them, listening stoically as Ryan filled him in on the couple's camper. For the first time in a long time, a thin smile teased at his lips. "I think Bundt just made his first big mistake. Folks, I'll call for a deputy to take you to a motel while we find your camper. Please wait inside where it's warmer."

"Just so you know, whoever took it won't get far. Radiator leaks pretty badly. Had an appointment in the morning to get it fixed." The man turned and pushed the cart back to the store, the woman at his side.

"Anything?" Ryan asked. He liked knowing the camper would be disabled soon.

"The store manager said he knew a car had been stolen, but that was it. No news of any other missing woman, but maybe we just haven't heard yet."

Ryan glanced in the direction of the road. "We need to find that camper."

"I agree. He won't be able to go fast. I'll contact the feds. Hopefully, they can get a chopper. Otherwise, it's fifty-fifty which direction he went."

Ryan jogged to his car, the sheriff following, and slid into the driver's seat. "Come on, which way?"

"Right there, Captain." The sheriff pointed to a trail of water leading from the lot. "Leaving crumbs like Hansel and Gretel."

Chapter Twenty-one

Lance peered around the camper as a car pulled up behind them and a young woman got out. He smiled and wiped his grubby hands on a dish towel he'd removed from inside. Stupid motorhome. He'd thought it the perfect way to transport Maddy until it overheated on his way back.

The woman didn't leave the side of her car. Instead, she held up her cell phone. Smart little thing. "Do you want me to call someone for you?"

"Do you have service? My phone is dead, and I really need to call my wife so she won't worry. May I use your phone?" He moved slowly toward her.

She moved to the other side of the car. "I'll slide it to you."

"That's fine." He kept his smile in place. The closer he got, the easier it was to see the dark roots in her dyed blond hair. Maybe he shouldn't stick to just blondes. Now that he had Maddy, all young women could feed his hunger. At least he could find out with this one.

Her eyes widened. "You're him."

Before Lance could react, she dove into her car and locked all the doors, tears running down her cheeks as she raced to roll up her window. She screamed as he shoved his hand through the space remaining. Her screams piercing his eardrums, she stabbed at his hand with her car keys until he withdrew.

She jammed the keys into the ignition and started the car.

Lance picked up a rock the size of his fist and slammed it against the window.

She screamed again and sped away, peppering him with pebbles.

Too many people had seen his face on the news. Now what? He stood in the middle of the road and contemplated his options.

He could try to highjack a car in hopes they wouldn't recognize him until it was too late. His grandmother's house was too far for him to walk.

A semi appeared over the slight hill. Truck drivers were on the road a lot. Maybe he wouldn't have seen the news.

Lance waved his arms over his head.

The truck slowed and stopped.

"Need a ride, buddy?"

"Sure do. Next town is where I need to go but don't relish walking ten miles."

"Not a problem. Hop in."

Lance grinned and climbed inside.

~

"A woman called saying she saw Bundt out on Highway 62 next to a broken-down motorhome." The sheriff strode from his office. "Miller, man the phones. Maxwell, you're with me."

Ryan jumped to his feet. "I'm sure he's long gone by now."

"Most likely. The woman is on her way here. Miller can take her statement. We'll speak to her later."

Ryan agreed. They couldn't waste time waiting on the caller. The two rushed to Ryan's car and sped to where the caller said she'd spotted Bundt. *Hold on, Maddy. I'm coming.*

The motorhome stuck out white against the dark winter trees lining the road. The hood stood open. The owners hadn't been wrong in saying the vehicle wouldn't get far.

Gun in hand, Ryan hitched his arm brace more securely on his shoulder and followed the sheriff into the motorhome. Empty. No sign of a victim, just a half-drunk can of soda in the console near the driver's captain's chair.

"Well…" The sheriff exhaled heavily. "He found a ride somehow."

Ryan watched a semi roar past. "The CB. Let the truckers know we're searching for him. If one of them picked him up, maybe they can detain him somehow."

"Unless they didn't take him far."

It was worth a shot. Ryan returned to his car and opened his trunk. He kept a CB there in case of emergencies. This warranted him hooking it back up.

Sheriff Westbrook chuckled. "I bet you were a boy scout as a kid."

"Always be prepared. I'll need your help since I only have one working arm." He stepped back so the sheriff could retrieve the equipment.

Half an hour later, Ryan had let every trucker within a specified radius know to be on the lookout for Bundt, giving a full physical description.

"Breaker, breaker." The CB crackled. "This is

Lonely Lion. I dropped off a man of that description a few minutes ago at the city limits of Forestville."

Ryan whipped to face the sheriff. "Was he alone?"

"Yep. Picked him up next to a motorhome on the highway."

"Did he say where he was headed?"

"To see his wife."

Ryan's heart dropped, then leaped with hope. If he thought of Maddy as his wife, maybe he didn't intend to kill her. "Thank you."

"Forestville is a rural town of farms spread out over several miles," the sheriff said. "The actual city center is small. A gas station, grocery store—that sort of thing. If Bundt is there, finding out which farmhouse will be next to impossible."

"Hey, we're getting closer with each second. We'll find them." Ryan set his revolving light on top of his car, turned on the siren, and sped toward Forestville ten miles away. Maddy was one of the smartest people he knew. She'd find a way to stay alive, to break free, and he'd be there when she did. They had to find her by tomorrow, just in case he was wrong about Bundt not killing her.

"You grip that steering wheel any harder and you'll break it." The sheriff laid a hand on his arm. "Relax and get us there in one piece. Somebody in that little town will have seen or heard something. We'll ask at the gas station first."

One thing about small towns was everyone knew everything that went on. If Bundt had stopped anywhere on his way to wherever he took Maddy, someone would remember.

He cut off the lights and sirens as they neared the

city limits. The lone gas station in town wasn't hard to spot. A cross junction with the station, a grocery store, and a volunteer fire department made up "downtown." A few fast food places lined the highway. Other than that, Forestville didn't have much.

Ryan pulled in front of the gas station.

"Wait here." Sheriff Westbrook opened his door. "I'll be back."

He returned a few minutes later. "A man fitting Bundt's description stopped for gas and paid at the pump. The only reason he was noticed was because the attendant was replacing the water for cleaning car windows."

"Was he alone?"

The sheriff shook his head. "The attendant said a pretty blond woman sat in the car." His phone rang. He answered and listened, a smile spreading across his face. "Bundt's grandmother owned land and a house on the outskirts of Forestville. The address is being texted to me."

~

Man, it was cold. Maddy shivered under the thin quilt, waiting for Lance to return so she could convince him to free her hands. With the door at the top of the stairs locked and the basement windows too narrow for her, she had no other alternative but to wait. She prayed her hands wouldn't be too cold to use the nail if she had to.

The lock on the door clicked. The door squeaked as it opened.

"Well, I've had a heck of a day," Lance said, descending the stairs. "I'm counting on you to brighten it up for me. Are you hungry?" He set a fast-food bag at the foot of the cot. "Chilly in here. I might need to get you a space heater."

Maybe she wouldn't be dead by the end of tomorrow. Of course, an attempt to escape might change things. "Thank you." Sliding the nail under the skinny pillow, she sat up, keeping the quilt around her shoulders. "Can I ask you something?"

"Anything." He tilted his head, a curious look in his eyes.

"Why three days?" She pulled a French fry from the bag and popped it into her mouth. Still hot. "What were you waiting for?"

"For them to show me whether they would be a good replacement for my Sarah."

"Your wife?"

He nodded. "We'd had a falling out. She wanted to leave me, get a divorce. I kept her here for three days. When she didn't come to reason, I...I made it look like a suicide in order not to lose my job."

The food stuck in her throat. "You killed her."

"I had to, don't you see?" He scratched the back of his neck. "Until you, no one came close to replacing her. You even look a lot like her. Tall, thin, long hair. I thought at first your sister would be the one, but she wouldn't love me. Do you love me?"

She forced her smile not to tremble. "I'm starting to. Will you kill me tomorrow if I don't?"

He frowned. "Can't answer that. I don't want you to love me just so I don't kill you."

Why else would she pretend to care? She fought to keep from rolling her eyes and pulled a cheeseburger from the bag. "That makes sense. There are things you can do to help me."

"Wait a minute," he growled. "You're untied."

"The tape was cutting off my circulation." She tried to appear nonchalant about it all. "I waited for you, didn't I?" Her heart thudded so hard she thought he'd hear it.

His shoulders relaxed a bit. "So, you did. May I sit closer?" He moved to the end of the cot and reached over to tuck her hair over her shoulder. "Don't hide your gorgeous face."

"Okay." It took all her strength not to shudder at his touch. Her hand snaked for the nail under the pillow.

"May I kiss you? I've dreamed of our lips meeting from the first moment I saw you. I wanted to when I took you out to supper, but you shied away. I admired that. Means you're moral. I'd like to...do more, here on the cot, if you'd let me. You'd know for sure whether you love me if we...became one." His gaze searched her face.

"No." She shook her head and scooted back.

His face darkened. "I'll *take* it from you then. You'll be mine. The captain will no longer want you." He shoved her on her back, tossing aside the quilt, and leaned over her.

Her hand gripped the roofing nail.

He plastered his lips on hers.

She plunged the nail into his neck. Warm blood spurted, covering them both with its stickiness.

Shoving him aside, Maddy gagged, swiping her sleeve across her eyes and scrambled for the stairs.

With a roar, Lance lunged for her, gripping her ankle.

Her kick to his face knocked him back. He fell to

the dirt floor of the basement. "I will kill you, Madison!"

Not waiting to see if he'd come after her, she thundered up the stairs and out the front door. The frigid night air slapped her. She wrapped her arms around her middle and continued her mad dash for the road.

Someone would come. Someone would drive by.

She spared a quick glance behind her. No sign of Lance. Had she killed him? Knocked him unconscious? She wouldn't go back to find out. Maddy stopped at the edge of the highway and glanced both ways. Not a single headlight pierced the growing darkness. Which way should she go? Think. She hadn't been blindfolded.

A dead tree on her left brought back the thought of how she'd thought it would make a great black and white photograph. She turned left, continuing to run until her breath came in gasps. She bent at the waist and tried to regulate her breathing.

Headlights appeared over a rise. She straightened and waved her arms.

The car stopped a few feet away.

"Maddy?" Ryan rushed toward her, pulling her close. "Are you hurt? Where?"

"It's not my blood." She gave directions to Lance's grandmother's house. "I don't want to go back, Ryan." She clutched the collar of his shirt.

"We'll wait in the car. The sheriff will check on Bundt." He helped her into the backseat of his car. "Sheriff, mind driving?"

"Nope."

Ryan slid in beside Maddy. "You're freezing."

"The basement was freezing." Her teeth chattered—from the bitter cold or shock, probably both.

Ryan removed his coat and wrapped it around her shoulders. "You'll be warm soon."

The sheriff pulled close to the house and got out of the car, his gun drawn.

Maddy watched through the front windshield as he entered the house. A few minutes later, he exited, phone to his ear. He had a short conversation with someone before returning to the car.

"You won't have to worry about Bundt anymore," he said. "He's dead, lying in a pool of his own blood. You stabbed that roofing nail right in his jugular."

Maddy dissolved into tears and buried her face in Ryan's chest.

Chapter Twenty-two

Maddy stood on the dock to say her last goodbyes. She wouldn't cry. Not anymore. She'd accomplished what she'd come to Misty Hollow for. Justice.

"I did it, Alli. The man who killed you is dead. No years behind bars. He'll never hurt anyone again. I'm sorry about your house, but I can't stay here anyway."

Which had become a constant ache in her heart over the last week. She'd answered a myriad of questions regarding her time with Lance. Gone with Ryan to pick up Danny and given her intent not to renew her contract at the elementary school. Misty Hollow held too much pain for her to stay. What would hurt the most, though, was leaving Ryan behind.

"Maybe we aren't meant to find love, sis. You'll never have a chance now, and my chances have flown away." She exhaled heavily, feeling more alone than ever.

It had once been she and Alli, two against the world. Now, Maddy faced the future alone.

She whirled at footsteps behind her.

Ryan stopped and held up his hands. "It's just me. I thought I'd find you here."

"You startled me. It'll take a while for me not to jump at sudden sounds."

"Mind if I join you? I'd like to talk to you about something."

She glanced once more at the calm surface of the lake, then nodded. "The bench?"

"Sure." He held out his hand.

With only a slight hesitation, she placed her hand in his, pausing again at the bench where Lance had abducted her. It was only a bench. It couldn't harm her. She sat down before she changed her mind.

Ryan took a deep breath and turned her to face him. "I know you're leaving. I saw the for-sale sign where your sister's house once stood."

"I can't stay here. I just can't." The hated tears welled in her eyes. So much for no more crying.

"I understand." He cleared his throat. "I've given my notice at the department. I'm transferring to Langley's police force as a detective."

"That's great news for you." She forced a smile. "It hasn't been easy for you here either."

"I'm bumbling this." He took both her hands in his. "I want you to go with me. I love you, Madison. Please don't make me go through life without you."

Forget not crying. The tears now poured down her cheeks. "I don't want to go through life without you."

"Will you marry me?"

She nodded, so relieved she wouldn't be leaving him that she sagged against him. "I love you, Ryan. Of course, I'll marry you. What did Danny say?"

"I knew you'd wonder whether I spoke to him."

With the forefinger of his right hand, he tilted her face up to his. "Danny's excited. He said he'll have a mom and dad again, even if his new mommy is a teacher."

She closed her eyes as he lowered his head to kiss her. When they parted, breathless and cold from the winter wind, Maddy took one last glance at the lake. "Rest in peace, Alli. You'll always be in my heart."

The End

Read the first chapter of the next book, Lightning Never Strikes Twice.

Chapter One

One more room to clean, the boss's office, and Alisa Gosling could put the long, work-burdened day behind her. She'd taken on way too many jobs in her quest to own a house of her own. Somewhere away from the city. Somewhere perfect like a small town.

Alisa adjusted the earbuds as she listened to sea shanties and reached for the business owner's door. Opening it, she flicked on the light. The place looked clean, other than an overflowing trashcan. Still, she'd dust and polish it. She couldn't afford to lose her largest client.

After she finished dusting and her playlist looped back to the beginning, she reached for the trashcan. Several pages fell to the floor, joining an errant piece under the desk. Alisa dropped to her knees and reached as far as she could. Aha. Her fingers closed around the wayward pages.

She glanced down at the paper on top. It was a torn-up letter. Not handwritten but typed. If she hadn't spotted the words *corrupt* and *police*, she would've tossed the pages. Instead, her curiosity piqued, and she lay the sheets on the desktop and put them in order.

Ice water trickled down her spine. The letter was a

threat, exposing Mr. Barker, the construction business owner, of cutting corners and padding pockets. The sender went so far as to accuse Mr. Barker of bribing city officials and the police to look the other way. The writer promised to expose the entire thing.

A beep sounded, signaling someone exiting the elevator.

Alisa shoved the pages in her pocket, locked the office door, and scurried under the desk. She peered out, her heart in her throat.

A man's shadow paused in front of the door. She could see his cupped hands around his eyes as he peeked through the frosted glass.

Alisa held her breath. Her cleaning cart sat right outside the door. Whoever was out there would know she was in the office.

The door handle rattled.

Alisa gasped.

A key clicked in the lock.

Another voice from someone she couldn't see called the man away from the door.

After several tense minutes, Alisa crawled from under the desk, the papers in her pocket crinkling. She'd turn them over to the police the first chance she had.

Stuffing the rest of the garbage in her cart and putting a fresh plastic bag in the can, she took another long look around the room. In her haste to hide, she'd forgotten to turn off the lights. Whoever had stood on the other side of the door knew someone was in the room. Who other than the cleaning lady after hours?

She unlocked and opened the door. After peering up and down the hallway, she pushed her cart out. In an attempt to look innocent in case someone saw her, Alisa strolled nonchalantly toward the elevator, singing along with the song coming through her earbuds.

Outside the elevator on the first floor, two men, one of them Mr. Barker, stood near the reception desk in muffled conversation. Alisa smiled and kept on walking, hoping they couldn't hear how hard her heart beat.

Did one of them just call out to her? She wheeled her cart into the supply closet and grabbed the bags of garbage along with the supplies she carried back and forth. Without looking back, she kept singing and hurried out the back to the dumpster and her car.

Her hands started trembling so violently she could barely turn the key in the ignition. She backed from the space and sped away from the building. A glance in the rearview mirror showed Mr. Barker and the other man standing there watching as she drove away.

Why would someone be stupid enough not to shred such an incriminating document? Had Mr. Barker realized it hadn't been done and came back to make sure it had? Or was she jumping to conclusions?

A man as wealthy as Mr. Barker was sure to have enemies. People who accused him of all sorts of things. Maybe that's why he hadn't shredded the letter. He hadn't felt as if he needed to. Then why show up at the office well after eight p.m.? If he had more work to do, wouldn't he have simply stayed late?

She gave herself a mental shake as she pressed the garage door remote on the visor of her SUV and pulled in. As the door lowered behind her, she released the breath she'd been holding. Her shaky hands were the result of having read too many mystery novels. A business owner could show up at his business any time he wanted.

She set her purse and car keys on the kitchen island, poured herself a glass of sweet, sparkling wine, and settled in front of the television—her nightly ritual in order to wind down after a long day.

A news reporter stood in front of Barker Construction. Alisa turned up the volume in time to hear that a woman had been found dead and stuffed in a closet.

The hand holding her wine started shaking again. The woman turned out to be Mr. Barker's secretary. They weren't saying how she died, but the fact Mr. Barker had found her in a closet signified it hadn't been pleasant. As if murder ever was. And Alisa would bet her favorite pair of shoes the woman had been murdered.

Alisa couldn't wait until morning to turn over the letter to the authorities. She reached for her phone and called the police department who promised to send an officer over right away. Again, she put the pieces together on her kitchen table and snapped a photo with her phone. Just in case. When she wasn't pacing, Alisa peeked repeatedly through the blinds for someone to show up. Hopefully, the police and not someone who suspected she had the letter.

Relief swept through her like a burst of air when a van pulled in front of the apartment she rented, and a uniformed officer climbed out. She should never have taken the letter. Stupid.

A few moments later, a knock sounded at the door. Alisa opened it and ushered the officer in before locking the door again. "It's in pieces, but here it is."

He raised his eyebrows. "You say you found this in the garbage? Are you in the habit of digging through the trash bins of your clients?"

"No. I noticed it when a couple of the pages slipped out of the overflowing can and fell under the desk. I'd really convinced myself it meant nothing until watching the news tonight."

"Why would that matter?"

"Because a woman was killed either while I was cleaning—"

"Wouldn't you have heard something?"

She shook her head. "I wear earbuds and listen to music while I clean, so I never hear anything."

Why did she get the impression his shoulders relaxed at her response?

"I'm sure it's nothing, Miss Gosling. Thank you for bringing it to our attention." He nodded and helped himself out.

Peering through the blinds again, she watched him slide into his van.

The officer hadn't shown his badge, and now he stared through the windshield at her apartment. The streetlamp cast a shadow on his features. The part Alisa could see sent spiders along her skin. She let the blinds fall back into place.

The next day, that same dark blue van appeared in front of every house she cleaned. Surely, that wasn't coincidence.

Instinct told her she'd stumbled across something dangerous. That it was time to run as far from Westport as she could go. Rather than go to her last job, she headed home, taking care not to act suspicious. As per her routine, she pulled into the garage. Inside the house, she turned on the television which would flicker through the blinds.

Then, she turned on her laptop and searched for a sanctuary. A town called Misty Hollow sounded like just the place. Cradled in a valley, the town was surrounded by miles and miles of wooded forest. She found a small two-bedroom house for rent on some ranchland and jotted down the address. Alisa erased her browser history and slid her laptop into its bag. Then, she emptied her cabinets of all dry food and bottled water before heading to her room to pack.

How would she leave without being followed? She hurried to the front window. No sign of the blue van. All the cars out front belonged to her neighbors. So far so good. Maybe they'd decided she wasn't a threat after all. It didn't matter. Alisa wasn't sticking around to find out.

Behind the protection of the closed garage door, she loaded her vehicle with as many personal belongings as would fit, grateful for a large-model automobile. When she'd packed in as much as she could, she did a final run through of the apartment, filled a thermos with coffee, and then slipped into the driver's seat.

Alisa backed away from the house she'd rented for five years and sped toward the interstate. She cast many looks in her rearview mirror but didn't see anyone following her. Of course, she wouldn't unless they were obvious. She wasn't a detective in any sense of the word.

Thank goodness for the coffee. She didn't cross over the Misty Mountain into Misty Hollows until the sun started to peek over the top. Alisa glanced at her

GPS and drove slowly through the quaint little town, making note of the store signs, then continued down a country road. Five miles from town, she turned right onto a dirt road that passed under an arched sign announcing Leaning O Ranch and stopped in front of a sprawling ranch-style house. She'd arrived.

Alisa yawned and plodded onto the porch then rapped on the front door. A dog barked inside. A sleepy voice told it to hush.

A few seconds later, a man wearing plaid lounge pants and nothing else opened the door. A large mixed-breed dog with a brindle coat peered around his leg. "Yeah?" the man said.

Alisa cleared her throat. "I'd like to rent the house you listed online."

He blinked rapidly, then ran his hand through hair kissed with auburn on the ends. The bluest eyes she'd ever seen narrowed. "Why didn't you call first?"

"I was on the road." She tilted her head. "Is it available? I clean houses for a living. I could clean yours for a break in the rent. Either way, I'm here and need a place to stay."

He rubbed his hands briskly down his face. "The cabin is available. It's out back and unlocked. Can we talk about this once I've had a chance to wake up?"

"Of course." Alisa smiled. "I'll unload my bags. Thank you." Her steps perked up on the way to her SUV. She had a place to stay. The ad had said fully furnished, so as long as things were serviceable, they'd do just fine. She wasn't picky.

The house with white aluminum siding looked like something out of a magazine, inside and out. Inside, it had been decorated with blues and yellows. Clearly a woman had lived here at one time.

The master bedroom contained a queen-sized poster bed. The hours of driving and the stress of looking over her shoulder made her tired. Alisa lay on top of the quilt and fell asleep.

~

"Well, find her! Search every small town near here, then branch out to the surrounding states. She's a woman alone and wouldn't have gone far." He slammed the phone down, cracking the screen protector. The woman was only a cleaning lady. How smart could she be? He ought to have Barker killed along with his secretary. Stupid woman. Didn't she understand what a shredder was for?

If news got out about this, he'd be ruined. They had to find that cleaning lady.

Dear Reader,

Sometimes small towns carry secrets, hide evil people behind a façade of charm and happiness. I'm enjoying writing this series of strong men and women looking for a new life and finding danger and love along the way in a world where justice is always served.

If you enjoyed Calm Surface, please leave a review on Amazon. Reviews are important to authors and help get their books noticed by new readers.

God Bless,

Cynthia Hickey

Website at www.cynthiahickey.com

Multi-published and best-selling author, Cynthia Hickey, has taught writing at many conferences and small writing retreats. She and her husband run the publishing press, Winged Publications, which includes some of the CBA's best well-known authors. They live in Arizona and Arkansas, becoming snowbirds with two dogs and one cat. They have ten grandchildren who them busy and tell everyone they know that "Nana is a writer."

Connect with me on FaceBook
Twitter
Sign up for my newsletter and receive a free short story
www.cynthiahickey.com

Follow me on Amazon
And Bookbub

Made in the USA
Monee, IL
18 June 2024

60074852R00114